REQUIRED
TO WEAR THE
TYCOON'S RING

BY
MAGGIE COX

MILLS &
BOON

First published in Great Britain 2016
By Mills & Boon, an imprint of HarperCollins*Publishers*
1 London Bridge Street, London, SE1 9GF

ISBN: 978-0-263-26378-7

Was she going to tell him that she'd changed her mind about marrying him? When Seth realised it was a possibility he sensed his heart race in protest.

'What is it?'

'It's nothing… I just— I just…'

As she brushed aside her hair, where it glanced against her cheek, Imogen's gaze was surprisingly steady. Seth couldn't attest to the fact that he even breathed right then. The look in her eyes stopped all thought in its tracks. What he saw in those silken burnished depths was a seductive mix of desire, need and longing…all the things he'd secretly yearned for her to want from him and more…

'What are you trying to do to me?' he husked.

'Don't worry… I just want you to kiss me…'

Whether the gesture was meant, or purely unconscious, she moistened her heavenly shaped lips with her tongue.

'Is that allowed on the night before we get married, Seth?'

Maggie Cox is passionate about stories that can uplift and transport people out of their daily worries to a more magical place, be they romance novels or fairy tales. What people want most, she believes, is true connection. She feels blessed to be married to a lovely man who never fails to make her laugh, and has two beautiful sons and two much loved grandchildren.

Books by Maggie Cox

Mills & Boon Modern Romance

A Rule Worth Breaking
The Man She Can't Forget
The Tycoon's Delicious Distraction
In Petrakis's Power
What His Money Can't Hide
The Lost Wife
The Brooding Stranger
Mistress, Mother…Wife?
Surrender to Her Spanish Husband

Seven Sexy Sins

A Taste of Sin

The Powerful and the Pure

Distracted by Her Virtue

A Deal with the Devil

A Devilishly Dark Deal

One Night In…

One Desert Night

British Bachelors

Secretary by Day, Mistress by Night

Visit the Author Profile page at millsandboon.co.uk for more titles.

REQUIRED TO WEAR THE TYCOON'S RING

To my dear friend Mietzche for your love and support during a challenging time and your wonderful ability to make me laugh when I feel like crying! Maggie x

CHAPTER ONE

It doesn't matter how long it takes... I'll wait for you. No one is going to keep us apart. There's nobody else on this earth for me but you. You're the only one who can calm the lightning in my soul and help me find peace. If you ever doubt the strength of my love I want you to know that I love you more than life itself and always will...

IMOGEN READ THE words and it was as though they bled onto the page, such was the impact they conveyed. The depth and power of the sentiment pierced her heart, and something inside, something that had been tight and unyielding for so long, started to melt and unravel... Before she could stop it a stinging hot tear splashed down onto the once tightly folded piece of notepaper in her hand.

In her spare time she often browsed the charity shop shelves in the hope that she might find something new or interesting. The note she was reading had been carefully inserted inside the anthology of a well-known romance poet. As she'd flicked through the well-thumbed pages the unexpected addition had spilled out and revealed itself. The note had landed at her feet.

There was no indication of the writer's name, just the initials SB. Was the writer male or female? she wondered. All Imogen knew was that the poignant promise 'I'll wait for you' had her longing to experience being loved so deeply that she would never have cause to doubt that she was cared for.

Her recent excoriating experience of being jilted at the altar had almost entirely crushed any hope she had that there were men out there who were genuinely loving and considerate. Yet in a secret corner somewhere Imogen refused to relinquish that hope. Had the note's writer reconciled with his or her lover after whatever had torn them apart? she mused.

With a trembling sigh, she momentarily shut her eyes. It wasn't easy to deal with the tumult of the feelings that rolled through her. Sometimes they threatened to spill over and undermine what little confidence she had left.

She'd never experienced such loving devotion and she *longed* to. If only she could discover whether or not things had worked out well for the couple... It would mean so much to her if they had. She wanted evidence that hopes and dreams *could* be fulfilled and that true love *could* last so long as the lovers drew breath...

She made a resolve. Suddenly impatient, she finished her browsing. Carefully reinserting the note inside the book, she moved across to the cashier to pay.

The cheerful elderly assistant smelled liberally of lavender, and her pristine white blouse was perfectly ironed and starched, as though she wouldn't dream of leaving the house unless it was.

As she surveyed Imogen her face crinkled in a welcoming smile, just as if she was a trusted old friend. 'Found something nice, have you, dear?'

'Yes. I have. I'd like to buy this book,' she replied.

When the sale had been rung up on the till the woman put the purchase into a crumpled carrier bag.

After murmuring, 'Thanks...' as she took it, Imogen asked, 'By the way, can I ask if you know who donated the book? Only I was in here a couple of days ago and I didn't notice it on the shelves then...'

'I can't tell you who donated it, my dear, but I do know that my colleague took a delivery of books from the big house up on the hill yesterday. You must know the one I'm talking about—that splendid Gothic mansion that backs onto the woods? Evergreen, I think it's called. It used to belong to the Siddons family, but they're long gone now. I think there's somebody looking after the place but no one knows who. There's a rumour that it's been bought by some business corporation to use for staff training... You can always enquire. Does that help?'

Although Imogen smiled, the expression didn't come as easily to her as it had used to. She was sad about that. What she wouldn't give to return to the land of the living, with her heart whole again and the optimism she'd always managed to somehow find well and truly restored.

Clutching the carrier bag against the black bouclé jacket she'd discovered in another charity shop, she said, 'It does. Thanks for the tip.' Glancing across at the shop's thick glass doors, she added, 'Have a good day... It looks like the sun might come out if we're lucky.'

'It does, doesn't it? But it probably won't shine on us for very long. Still, I hope that won't spoil things for you. Perhaps reading some of those wonderful poems will help?'

As she walked back to the small flat she rented in a Victorian mid-terrace down a narrow side street, her route took her across the city's historic cobblestones, and Imogen automatically glanced towards the formidable cathedral that rose up before her. It was a real Mecca for tourists, but personally she found it intimidating.

To her eyes it spoke of too many spirits not at peace. She'd only explored it once, and it hadn't invited her for a second visit. If a person was hoping for comfort, would they honestly find it within those oppressive ancient walls? Somehow Imogen didn't think so.

The wind that was now gusting in earnest blew her hair haphazardly across her face. With a shudder she sensed an icy chill run down her back. So much for that promising glimpse of sunshine earlier! Winter was definitely starting to make itself felt. She couldn't wait to get back inside, light the wood burner and examine her book. Who knew? There might even be some further evidence about the identity of the original owner.

If there wasn't, she would love to dig a little deeper and find out. But even if she found the person, she realised that being confronted with such a note might potentially elicit some kind of unsettling repercussions for the person concerned. Her sigh was heavy. The story behind the poignant note was perhaps consuming her thoughts much more than it ought to...

Seth sat himself down on the wide mahogany staircase with its faded gold-trimmed runner and stared around him. The ticking of the old grandfather clock in the hall hypnotically marked the time, taunting him with the memories it scratched, as if he had deliberately dug his nails into an old, once infected wound and reopened it.

He had plenty of cause for being disturbed. The first time he had entered this house as a lad of nineteen he'd been full of trepidation at the thought of meeting his girlfriend's intimidating father because he was going to ask for her hand in marriage. The esteemed financier James Siddons had been known to put the fear of God even into his peers—let alone the hopeful boy from the wrong side of the tracks that Seth had once been.

Although he and Louisa had only been seeing each other for a couple of months, they'd known from the very first moment that they were meant to be together. What they'd felt for each other had gone far deeper than simple attraction. But he had known the path they'd planned to take wasn't going to be easy. She'd still been a student at the university, and Seth an apprentice car mechanic at a local dealership. Hardly of the material to render him acceptable to her esteemed family.

He'd had to garner every ounce of courage he had in him on the day of the meeting. And every one of his fervent hopes to make a good impression had been utterly dashed as soon as he'd laid eyes on the stern-faced banker. He'd barely even crossed the threshold before the man had very candidly expressed his dislike. And when Seth had bolted his courage to the floor, met his gaze eye to eye and confidently declared that he wanted to marry his daughter, he had been immediately shot down and put in his place.

'Louisa knows perfectly well that families like ours

marry into families from the same class, Mr Broden. And clearly you are *not* from that class, so there's no sense in beating about the bush, is there? My advice to you is to stick with your own kind,' Siddons had finished.

'You're not even giving him a chance!' Louisa had burst out. 'I love him. I want no one else. You have no right to put him down like that and make him feel small. Seth has nothing to be ashamed of. He came round to speak to you because he wanted to do things properly. We could just as easily have sneaked off and done the deed without telling you, but it was Seth who insisted we should do the right thing and be upfront about it.'

Appalled, James Siddons had issued her with a warning glare. 'I don't know what you thought you were playing at by encouraging a "nobody" like him,' he'd said. 'You must know that one day you'll have to marry someone suitable so that the family's lineage can continue. You are the last Siddons in the line, Louisa, and that makes it even more important for you to choose your husband wisely. I insist that you bring this charade with this man to an end right now. If you don't I will make sure that every penny of your allowance is frozen until such time as you do as I say.'

That day—that bittersweet day when they had sought to get Louisa's father's approval to marry— the man had broken his daughter's heart with his chillingly cold refusal. Seth would have done anything to spare her the disappointment and heartache that had followed, but his own heart had hardened like ice at James Siddons's brutal reception.

However, he had refused to let the rejection crush

him. So he was a *nobody*, was he? Squaring his already broad shoulders, he hadn't been able to contain his temper. Swearing that he would show James Siddons what a fool he was for believing that he was somehow better than Seth—just because he had gone to the right schools and his family had money—he had finally vented his spleen.

There would come a time soon when he would surpass James Siddons's wealth and power with his own, he'd vehemently told him, and Louisa would never have so much as one moment's worry about how they would survive.

But at the end of that cold encounter the supercilious banker had banned her from seeing him again, told him he would put a watch on her to make sure she kept to the command he'd declared, and he had threatened Seth with what he would be able to do if he should dare have the effrontery to try to persuade her differently.

'There won't be one dealership in the country that will hire you after what I tell them,' he'd finished.

With tears pouring down her face, Louisa had been able to do nothing else but urge Seth to go...

He sucked in a harsh breath and slowly released it. Why had he bought this place and opened up old wounds that should have long ago healed and scarred? He had nothing left to prove.

James Siddons had been dead for about a year now and—to his everlasting distress—Louisa had died not long after that volatile meeting with her father, having been mown down by a hit-and-run driver. It had been the most colossal shock, and Seth had honestly thought he would never get over it.

When the mansion had come on to the market not long after its owner's demise, six months ago, Seth hadn't been able to resist buying it. How could he have? It was the place where Louisa had grown up. He had an important personal connection with the place. Despite the house's dauntingly grand appearance, she'd confided to him that it had once been a very warm and loving home, thanks to her mother, Clare Siddons.

'My mother was a wonderful woman. She was infinitely patient and kind, and she always told me to follow my heart...not just my head,' Louisa had told Seth. 'She certainly wouldn't have looked down her nose at you because you come from the "wrong" background. She would only have had to look at you to know why you have my heart.' Her pansy-blue eyes had sparkled tenderly as she'd related that.

Now the atmospheric house she'd grown up in couldn't help but carry the beguiling remnants of her presence. Although his decision to buy it was no doubt a double-edged sword—one that could just as soon wound him as satisfy his urge to show the local community that he was just as good as his nemesis James Siddons. Seth wondered if he'd been led purely by his ego to buy it.

Ten long years had passed since Louisa's death—wilderness years in which Seth had distanced himself as far from his hometown as he could in order to rebuild his life without her—and he'd achieved everything he'd set out to do. He ought to let the past lie.

Yes, there had been other women after he'd lost Louisa, but throughout all the time that had passed he had never loved anyone else and most likely never would.

Buying the house had probably been a completely dumb idea. Talk about rubbing salt into his wounds!

Cursing himself as a masochist, then feeling certain he could always sell it if things didn't work out, he shoved to his feet and turned to go into the drawing room. It was now completely devoid of the once grand furniture that had filled it.

Louisa had once shown him the room when her father had been away on business. But by the time Seth had come to buy the place all that had been left were a few old books and some kitchen items. Everything else had been removed by the lawyers acting for her father—sold off to pay death duties.

As painfully ironic as it was, it turned out that James Siddons had not been nearly as wealthy as he'd claimed. Apparently he'd squandered his wealth on gambling and living the high life after Louisa had died.

Now the palatial room in front of him put him in mind of a ball that was at an end, with the well-heeled partygoers never to return. The only material items left in the lofty room were the faded red-and-gold carpets and the crimson velvet curtains that hung at the windows.

The day he'd accompanied Louisa in order to ask her father's permission to marry her he hadn't travelled any further than the imposing hallway. As Seth had anticipated James Siddons had hardly rolled out the welcome mat... Far from it. Instead, he'd straight away gone into attack.

He smiled grimly. Perversely, Seth was the one who had the last laugh. Now he had the satisfaction of knowing he was free to do what the hell he liked here.

Never again would he be accused of not being 'good enough' by someone who had been born with the proverbial silver spoon in his mouth, who hadn't had to rely solely on his own ability and wits to rise higher in the world, to make it against all the odds as Seth had. *He* was the one who owned the house now.

In the midst of his reverie a sudden inexplicable instinct drew him to the windows. He caught his breath when his eyes settled on the figure of a young woman in the fading light. She was peering through the wrought iron gates. He froze for a moment, thinking she was a ghost. When common sense swiftly returned he wondered irritably, just who did she think she was spying on the house?

Not thinking twice about finding out, Seth strode from the drawing room and went straight to the front door. Opening it wide, he took the carved granite steps two at a time, his boot heels crunching across the gravel. The woman had started to back away, but he halted her with the demand, 'Who are you and what do you want here?'

His visitor's startled brown eyes showed her shock and surprise. Just then her curling chestnut hair was blown wildly across her face by a rogue gust of wind, and her slender fingers visibly trembled as she pushed the strands away. For a mesmerising, unguarded moment Seth was transfixed by the delicacy and haunting loveliness of the features in front of him—so much so that it threw him off-kilter for a moment.

'Well?' When he next spoke—having decided not to be so easily beguiled by the woman, and realising she was probably just one of the bevy of journalists that tracked his career, looking for a story—his voice was terse.

'I'm sorry... I didn't mean to bother you.'

Her voice was soft as summer rain and added to the sense that she was casting a spell on him.

Seth sucked in a breath. 'But you *are* bothering me. Answer my question. What's your business here?'

For a couple of seconds the woman didn't seem to know. Then she said hesitatingly, 'I— Are you the house's owner?'

'What's it to you? Why do you want to know?'

'I'll tell you...but if you *are* the owner I wonder if I might have a word?'

Seth's cobalt blue eyes narrowed suspiciously. 'What about?'

'About the history of the house... My name is Imogen, by the way... Imogen Hayes.'

'And you want to know because...? Let me guess— you're *fascinated* by old historic houses and you intend to study this one for a school project?'

Underneath her pale skin the girl blanched. 'I'm hardly a schoolgirl. I'm twenty-four!'

'Who are you, then? Someone from the local newspaper?' he quizzed.

She grimaced. 'No. Look, if you *are* the new owner, could you perhaps spare me a couple of minutes? I promise I won't take up too much of your time.'

Even as everything inside him told him it was a bad idea—the girl probably *was* from the local newspaper, hoping to write an article about him along the lines of 'poor boy made good'—he took longer than he meant to in deciding what to do.

Having made his fortune in America, and returned

home a billionaire, Seth knew that his name couldn't help but arouse local interest. This girl probably wouldn't be the only interested party. But because he couldn't help admiring her pretty face, and the unexpected spark of attraction it had aroused in him, he decided to relent and let her in. What had he got to lose? If the piece turned out to be defamatory he wouldn't hesitate to sue the newspaper.

'You'd better follow me inside.'

He pulled opened the iron gates, and the grating sound they released set his teeth on edge.

The brunette quickly edged past him. 'Thank you. That's very good of you.'

'Are you sure? Goodness isn't something I'm generally known for,' he quipped drily.

A corner of what he could see was a pleasingly pretty mouth nudged in an unsure dimple before she glanced away and followed him across the gravel.

When they reached the front door a blast of cold air along with a couple of dried, burnished leaves flew in from the driveway to accompany them.

Seth frowned as he closed the door behind them. Answering her questions wouldn't take long, he was sure. In truth he knew very little about the house's history other than that it had been in Louisa's family for generations. So why on earth had he broken his own rule to be wary and instead invited the woman inside? Was it really because it had been too long since he'd been genuinely attracted to a woman and he'd found the opportunity too good to miss?

'I would suggest we talk in the living room, but as yet there isn't any furniture. I'm only here to look round today. You were lucky to find me in.'

'But you *are* the new owner?' The girl's even white teeth nervously clamped down on her fulsome lower lip.

'Yes, I am. Don't worry...I haven't invited you in under false pretences.' Combing his tawny hair back with his fingers, Seth made a half-hearted attempt at a smile. A sense of bitterness had seeped into his tone. The memory of James Siddons not thinking him good enough to cross his threshold, let alone marry his daughter, still had the power to sting even after all these years...

'I wouldn't dream of thinking anything like that. Perhaps you could tell me who you are?'

'My name is Seth Broden. What else do you want to ask me, Miss Hayes?'

Curling a strand of lightly waving rich brown hair round her ear, Imogen didn't hide her relief that he wasn't going to change his mind and tell her he'd made a mistake—that he didn't have time for her questions after all.

Whether by luck or design, her spontaneous evening stroll had skirted the imposing manor house, and when she'd spied its impressive turrets reaching up into the sky she hadn't been able to deny herself the impulse to take a closer look. At the back of her mind she'd been hoping for just such an opportunity, and that was why she carried the book with the note inside with her.

'I heard from someone local that the previous owner's family was called Siddons?'

The heavy thud of her heart was close to painful when she saw a guarded glint of steel invade his eyes, but she still couldn't help being drawn to him. The man's charismatic good looks had made her catch her breath as soon as she'd seen him up close. Acting purely on instinct, she had decided to stay and find out who he was…

'Yes…it was. You heard right.'

'And you knew them? I mean, you knew them when they lived here?'

'Why do you want to know? I presumed it was the house that you were interested in.'

'I am, but it's the people who make a house into a home…no matter how grand or intimidating it might be.'

Seth's brow furrowed. 'You think this place is intimidating?'

The girl reddened. 'Yes, I do, but only because it's so far removed from my own life. I can't envisage what it must have been like for anyone who lived here and could afford to run a place like this.'

'Having great wealth isn't all roses, you know. It doesn't change who you are fundamentally, be it bad or good. Look…this is all rather pointless. I don't think I can help you after all. If there's anything else you want to know, then I suggest you do some research at the local records office.'

'The information I'd like to find out is more of a personal nature, Mr Broden. I'd be so grateful if you could help.'

'I'm sure you would… But if there's one thing I've learned it's that the answers to life's questions don't always reveal themselves so easily, Miss Hayes.'

Guilt combined with an uncomfortable feeling of embarrassment washed over Imogen. She wondered if she'd come across as being insensitive. 'I know that, but… Can you perhaps tell me why the family moved away?'

'You could say that fate stepped in and took them down a very different path from the one they expected…'

Seth Broden's voice was huskily pitched and his gaze held hers unflinchingly. It was becoming very evident that he was in no hurry to reveal what he knew about the Siddons family, and Imogen quickly intuited that she'd have to tread carefully if she wanted to learn the truth about the note in her book.

'That holds true for a lot of us, I'm sure. The dreams we have don't always come to fruition.'

'I take it that's been your own experience, Miss Hayes?'

His comment took her aback. But she wasn't ready to share the events of her life that had taken *her* down an 'unexpected path' with a complete stranger—no matter how much his seductively handsome face and glittering blue eyes might compel her to. She should know by now the dire consequences of trusting people too easily, and if she didn't, she really *was* in trouble…

'Like most people, my life hasn't always gone smoothly.'

There was a flash of what looked to be empathy in Seth Broden's eyes. Folding his arms across his impeccable wool coat, he sighed. 'But you're young enough not to become cynical about the cards you've been dealt and you can move on. At least you have that in your favour.'

Surprised by the remark, Imogen shrugged. For a long moment it was hard to duck the beguiling blue gaze that suggested he would have no trouble in persuading any woman to share her innermost secrets.

Just who *was* this man? If it was true that he owned the mansion, he had to be someone important. There was an air of exclusivity about him that said if a situation called for it *he* would be the one taking charge.

If only she'd thought a bit longer about giving in to her impulse to look at the house. But after talking to the assistant at the charity shop she hadn't been able to resist. Having viewed it, she'd found the imposing and beautiful facade had piqued her curiosity even more.

'I'm sure you're right. Trouble is that's harder to do than you might imagine...'

'Then, my advice to you, Imogen, is to focus on the things that you *can* do and not worry about the rest. Now, are you going to tell me the true reason for your visit, because I sense that researching the family who lived here isn't the real reason why you're here.'

Seth Broden had stopped Imogen in her tracks on two counts. First by so familiarly using her name, and second by instinctively seeming to know that the reason for her interest in the Siddonses' family history was specific.

She realised she'd become more than a little possessive about the note, and didn't easily want to relinquish it. That was, not until she found out who its author was. She was uneasy. She realised she would have to tell him about it, even if it meant he demanded she return it.

'The other day I bought something from a local charity shop,' she began. 'I was told it had come from here. They'd taken delivery of a box of books from the house.'

Not commenting, Seth walked across to the window next to the door with a distinctly unhurried gait and stared out. What was he thinking about? He was still not saying anything, and his closed-off demeanour hardly suggested he was eager to break the silence.

The formidable quiet that ensued started to worry her. She was just about to ask if anything was the matter when he suddenly snapped out, 'So you found a book...? Care to tell me the title?'

With a helpless shiver Imogen hugged her arms over her coat. 'It's a book of love poems by William Blake.'

'Is it, indeed? You admire his work, do you?'

When Seth turned to face her she was mesmerised. The carved contours of his face might have been fashioned out of marble, they were so still. There was no expression in them whatsoever...*none*. And yet the burning blue of his eyes was fierce...

'Yes, I do...very much.'

'I once knew someone else who was fond of his poetry.'

The admission came out of the blue, and stunned Imogen because she hadn't expected it.

'Was it someone who lived at the house?' The question was out before she could check it.

'It might have been. Wasn't the owner's name in the book?'

'No, it wasn't. There was only—'

The man in front of her raised a dark eyebrow interestedly. 'You were going to say, Miss Hayes...?'

Fearing she'd said too much too soon, Imogen parried the question with another one of her own. 'Was the person who enjoyed Blake's poetry a woman?'

'You didn't answer my question.'

Her companion's lightly lined forehead warningly grew tighter, and it was easy to sense the shield that had slammed down into place. But no shield—however strong and impenetrable—could hide the truth. It was right at that instant when Imogen remembered the initials that had signed off the note—SB.

The person who'd written in such beguiling and heartfelt tones was Seth Broden himself...

CHAPTER TWO

SETH IMMEDIATELY SAW what he took to be dawning re-alisation on Imogen's face. He didn't know why, but his heart started to pound.

'Do you have the book with you? I'd like to take a look if you have,' he said.

The sigh that escaped her was no more than a whis-per but he heard it easily. The melting brown eyes be-fore him were fused to his for the longest moment, and he wondered the reason behind it. Then, delving down into her shoulder bag, she produced a compact yellow book without a jacket. Flicking through the pages, she carefully extracted a piece of paper. Not knowing why, he caught his breath.

Crossing the floor, she handed him the note.

'What's this?'

'It was inside the book when I bought it.'

Seth's insides clenched hard as a painful sense of knowing gripped him. Seconds later his glance fell upon the words he had written all those years ago.

The realisation that Louisa had kept his message inside the pages of her favourite poetry book was bit-tersweet. He hardly knew what to think, what to feel.

He had sent the note to her at the university, to make

sure she received it. They hadn't met since that humiliating meeting with her father.

She'd been utterly distraught when she had realised there was no hope that he'd consent to them being together—'not even if World War III is threatened!' That was how intransigent the man had been.

As all her hopes had seemingly turned to dust she hadn't been able to hide her sorrow. Before Seth had been able to reassure her that nothing would break them apart, she'd mouthed a forlorn *I'm sorry*, then quickly fled upstairs. He'd hardly known what to do.

After that, things had just gone from bad to worse. Once again he'd tried to get Siddons to relent and see sense but it had been useless. The man had been about as flexible as an iron wall. There had been no 'give' in his heart whatsoever.

Seth had slammed out through the door in a temper, vowing again that no matter what he and Louisa were going to be together. The pompous banker could do his worst, but Seth *would* find a way.

The next day he'd left Louisa this note at the university, because before he'd left the house her father had cruelly declared that he was confiscating her phone. To leave her a note had been Seth's only means of reaching her until he'd figured out something better. One thing was for sure: Siddons would burn the missive if he found it first.

But a few days later his whole world had shifted on its axis and been demolished, all his hopes and aspirations turned to rubble. A friend of Louisa's had knocked on his door in the early hours of the morning to inform him tearfully that she'd been killed in a hit-and-run accident. Seth had wanted to die, too. Just how was he going to carry on without her?

Now, tightly clutching the note, he walked across to the staircase and sank down onto one of the steps. He knew that it should comfort him to know that Louisa had read the message before she died and briefly treasured it, but he had been waiting too long to find that out, and in the meantime the damage had been done.

All that seeing it had done was reaffirm the fact that he should have tried harder to be with her, *much* harder... Even if her unrelenting father had come up with some trumped-up reason to prosecute him and had him thrown into jail.

Feeling enraged, he muttered a furious curse.

Watching Seth, Imogen felt two things hit her at once. The man was distraught. The repercussions that she had been wary of had come to pass. The muscle that flickered at the side of his lean, carved jaw immediately informed her that he was having significant trouble in containing his emotions. One thing was certain—seeing the note hadn't given him any pleasure.

That led to her next realisation. He and his loved one *hadn't* stayed together. No matter how much she'd hoped, true love *hadn't* sustained them after all. She felt like crying.

But her deep sense of disappointment was quickly overridden by her concern for the man sitting on the stairs. Leaning towards him, she gently laid her hand on his shoulder. 'Are you okay?'

Even as the words left her lips Imogen knew the question was futile.

Turning his haunted blue eyes towards her, Seth Broden's mouth twisted grimly. 'Meaning, am I still breathing and alive despite the fact that I probably should have gone to hell for my part in what happened?'

Contemptuously jerking his head, he stood up and shook off her hand.

'I need a drink.'

Imogen turned pale. Outside, the fierce wind battered against the leaded windows as if it would break through the glass. Suddenly she felt as though freezing jagged ice had invaded her veins. What did he mean by such a statement? Had something terrible happened?

Why hadn't she really thought about the wisdom or lack of it in contacting the note's author? Because now that she had found him it seemed to have delivered anything *but* happiness to him. Not meaning to, she'd blundered in regardless and brought pain to this man. As to what she'd achieved for herself—she'd just smothered another longed-for dream.

'I didn't know that the note would upset you so much,' she stated huskily. 'The message was so heartfelt. I just wanted to find out if—if the people involved had been reunited?'

'And what...? Prove that happy-ever-after really exists?'

Feeling as though she'd been whipped, Imogen flinched. 'What's wrong with that?'

Seth stared. 'I don't mean for you to come crashing back down to earth with a bang, sweetheart...but it's probably better if you don't delude yourself.'

'I'm guessing that *you* wrote the note?'

'Yes, I did.'

'I don't mean to intrude more than I've done already, but will you— Can you tell me what happened?'

He moved down the stairs to stand in front of her, his expression a mixture of anger and resignation, and she didn't know why he didn't demand she leave.

'The lady died...end of story.'

But Imogen saw that it wasn't the end of the story. How *could* it be?

'I'm so sorry.'

She meant it with all her heart. It was only natural that she'd commiserate with his loss. It honestly grieved her that fate had intervened and stolen the couple's happiness. God knew it was hard enough to come by.

Seth Broden wore the scars of that loss as if they were physical ones. They weren't easy to hide in such a compellingly carved face. Amidst such perfection the smallest irregularity couldn't fail to show.

'How did it happen?'

'It was a hit and run. The bastard didn't waste his time waiting to see what he'd done. Just left her lying in the road.'

'Dear God...' The shock ricocheted right through her.

Seth's tormented glance seared hers. 'No amount of condolence or sympathy is going to bring her back, so don't get upset on my account. Is your car outside?' he added sharply.

'I didn't drive. I walked here.'

'I take it you must live in town, then? That's about five miles away. Clearly a long walk doesn't faze you?'

Imogen shook her head. 'Not at all... I love it. It helps to keep me fit.'

'Even so, I'll give you a lift home. It's getting late as well as becoming dark.' He briefly glanced down at his watch. 'I never meant to stay here so long.'

She wasn't going to argue. She felt strangely reluctant to leave him. Perhaps on the way he might relent and tell her a little bit more about the woman he'd lost?

'So long as you're sure you're ready to leave?'

'I am. I was checking things over, but I'm finished now.'

'Are you going to move in here soon?'

'I haven't decided.'

'Oh. Well, I'm ready to go when you are, then.'

She swept back her silky brown hair and pulled the collar of her coat more snugly round her neck...not that it would give her much added protection against the wind that was howling outside. It sounded as if it was brewing up a cyclone!

They hurried out to his car. When they were ensconced in the sumptuous leather of Seth's comfortable sedan, he turned to her and said, 'Where to?'

As soon as Imogen gave him the directions he nodded in acknowledgement. 'I know exactly where you mean.' His expression failed to tell her whether the knowledge pleased him or not.

Leaving the impressive Gothic building behind them, they headed out through the tree-lined lanes towards the centre of the town. During the journey they were both silent. Imogen didn't feel quite brave enough to question him again, and she wanted to respect his need for what must be quiet reflection.

Just twenty minutes later they arrived, and Seth negotiated the roads that took them to her address. As instructed, he pulled up in front of a neat black door with a gilt number one on it. It was dusk, and a lone street lamp helpfully illuminated the small row of terraced houses. Apart from the ethereal soughing of the wind, all was quiet. Most of the town's workforce had departed for home.

Turning towards her companion, Imogen breathed out a sigh. Seth's expression was as implacable as ever, but his strong, lean hands gripped the leather-clad steering wheel as though it was a much-needed anchor.

She was sorry they hadn't had more time to talk. But, clutching at yet another straw, she said quickly, 'Can I offer you a drink...in payment for the ride home, I mean?'

'You think the age-old remedy of a cup of tea might help to set things right?'

The tone of his voice registered his scorn.

Pushing his fingers agitatedly through his hair, he continued, 'I don't want payment, but if you're going to offer me a drink, then I'd prefer something stronger than tea.'

She sensed her cheeks flush heatedly as his intense blue eyes roamed her face. It made it doubly hard to form a reply. 'I—I have some brandy that a friend bought me for my birthday. Will that do?'

'Yes, it will—but only if you agree to join me. I won't be making any more revelations, if that's what you're thinking, but a companionable silence might be welcome.'

Flushing again, Imogen nodded. 'All right, then. Why don't you park the car and come in? I'll leave the front door open. My flat is on the ground floor.' The words were out before she could stop them.

After unlocking the door, she entered the house. The small apartment she rented was easily accessible and the door opened onto a cosy, compact living room. She was putting a match to the tinder in the wood burner when she sensed Seth coming in behind her. Out of the corner of her eye she saw his interested gaze scan the room.

As was her habit, she'd left everything tidy that morning. The task helped her to get clear about the day ahead. But strangely the ability seemed to elude her now, as her glance collided with Seth's. Suddenly she didn't feel clear about very much at all. And ever since she'd laid her hand on his shoulder to comfort him the oddly intimate sensation of warmth and strength hadn't left her. It didn't help that she still sensed his agitation. The note she'd found had clearly been a great shock to him.

'Why don't you sit down?' she invited. 'I'll get you that drink.'

'Sure...' he murmured, shrugging off his coat.

He draped it over the arm of a nearby easy chair as though it was nothing, but she glimpsed the Italian designer label attached to the silk lining. The garment was both exclusive and expensive, and it said much about the taste of its owner.

She watched thoughtfully as he dropped down onto the battered brown leather couch that had serviced several other tenants before Imogen. Even though she'd personalised it with the flowing red-and-gold Indian shawl that she'd draped over the back, it was still more 'shabby chic' than smart. Positioned next to the couch was a pile of hardback books on a maple-wood coffee table, and he picked up the top one to examine it.

'Interesting,' he murmured, reading the flyleaf. 'I can see that you like a mystery.'

'Thrillers aren't really my thing, but a friend lent it to me,' she explained. 'She said the story was terrific.'

'Would that be the same friend who gave you the bottle of brandy?'

'Yes, it was, as a matter of fact...though I rarely drink that stuff at all. She was hoping I'd let my hair down and celebrate for once.'

Imogen stared at the fire and felt her cheeks heat. Why had she told him *that*?

'And did you?'

'I did—but not with brandy. I stuck to orange juice that night.'

Checking that the flame had taken hold in the wood burner, she straightened and dusted her hands down her jeans.

Her companion was studying her intently and, feeling strangely as if she'd been put under a spotlight, she said, 'Give me a minute and I'll go and get you that drink.'

The tiny kitchen was adjacent to the living room. It wasn't particularly well-appointed, but it had a fairly new gas stove, an original butler's sink that was still in good order, a plum-coloured granite worktop and a couple of sturdy pine shelves on which she'd stacked some blue-and-white crockery. The bottle of brandy was located next to the stoneware bread crock.

Pouring a proper drink for a man wasn't something she was remotely used to. Her ex-fiancé, Greg, had been teetotal. That was until she'd found out that he *wasn't*. It had been another lie amongst the many that he'd told her. But dwelling on the thought was apt to remind her of his shocking betrayal and make her mood plummet. She was determined not to let that happen. After all, she'd vowed to make a fresh start, hadn't she? From now on she wanted to believe that good things *did* and *could* happen, despite the evidence to the contrary. How else was she going to turn her life around?

But her hand visibly trembled as she reached for the bottle of brandy and she had to take a couple of deep breaths to steady herself. Seth Broden was the first man she'd ever invited back to the flat and she shouldn't forget that he was neither a friend nor a colleague. *He was practically a stranger*. And such was the contrast between the awe-inspiring mansion he owned and the modest flat she rented that it was bound to make her conscious of the difference between her life and his.

She reached up to the overhead shelf and retrieved a couple of glass tumblers and, taking the bottle of brandy with her, returned to the living room. Handing one of the glasses to Seth, she set the brandy down on the table beside him.

'Please help yourself. I'm just going to hang up my coat. Want me to do the same for yours?'

He quirked what looked to be an amused eyebrow and said, 'Thanks.'

When Imogen returned from hanging the garments on the coat stand the fire in the burner was nicely warming the room and, having helped himself to brandy, Seth had set down the book he'd been perusing. He'd also settled himself more comfortably on the couch. His hard-muscled legs were noticeably long in the smart black chinos he wore, she saw, and the width of his shoulders was impressive.

She would have had to be blind not to notice that fact. His girlfriend must have loved the sense of strength he exuded. No doubt it had made her feel protected.

'I've poured you a drink,' he said as she sat down in the chintz-covered armchair. 'Perhaps you'll make an exception tonight and join me?'

'Sure.' Taking a tentative sip, she felt the slow burn of alcohol register in her gut as she swallowed it down. It was so powerful it immediately brought tears to her eyes.

'You're not used to drinking at all, are you?' His tone was gently teasing.

Imogen felt like an idiot. A sophisticated woman she was *not*. Setting down her glass, she curled some of her hair round her ear. 'No…I'm not.'

Thankfully, her guest didn't pursue the topic. 'So, tell me, how long have you lived here?' he asked instead.

Trying to relax, she somehow found a smile. 'About a year.'

'And you work in the area?'

'Yes, I do.'

Still cradling his drink, Seth leaned forward. The movement stirred the air with the scent of his arresting cologne. She didn't know what made it smell so alluring but she didn't have to… It had got her attention.

'And what is it that you work at?'

'I'm a secretary. I work for a legal practice.'

'And you enjoy it?'

'As a matter of fact, I do. I'm lucky enough to work

for a very nice woman, and the work is genuinely interesting.'

'I'm glad to hear it. I think if everyone enjoyed their work the world would go a long way to being a better place. I recently read that eighty per cent of the population hate their jobs. Thank God I'm not one of those. It's bad enough having to deal with all the other challenges that can come at you.'

'What do you mean, exactly?'

'I mean like pain and disappointment and the death of loved ones. Yes, all that can grind even the most stoic person down.'

He took a generous swig of brandy, and to Imogen's surprise she saw a sudden flare of pain in his diamond-bright eyes. His doleful words reminded her of the reason they had met—why he happened to be sitting there in her flat. Her heart squeezed in sympathy.

'I agree. Life can seem unbearable sometimes. But we should never lose hope that things can get better.'

'I admire your optimism, Imogen. Long may it last.'

Her guest looked to be candidly assessing her, and she suddenly found herself transfixed by him. What would it be like to have such a charismatic man's regard? she wondered.

Fearing she was becoming too entranced, she said quickly, 'Anyway, you said that you appreciated a companionable silence and I've already been talking too much...'

'Not necessarily. Your voice is actually very soothing.'

Taken aback by the compliment, she said quickly, 'I've just remembered I've got a couple of things to do in the kitchen. Do you mind if I leave you on your own for a while?'

'Not at all… That is, unless you'd prefer to stay and talk to me?'

Such a simply put invitation shouldn't make her insides flutter with the most intoxicating pleasure but it *did*, and her reaction warned her to tread very carefully where Seth Broden was concerned.

'I don't have a preference, but I perfectly understand if you want some time on your own for a while. Just call me if you need anything.'

Seth blinked and glanced away. 'As tempting as that offer sounds, sweetheart, there's nothing I really need right now other than the brandy.'

'I'll leave you in peace, then.'

His gaze immediately found hers again and he looked far from reassured. 'Not possible—but I appreciate the sentiment.'

Even as she left the room Imogen remembered the note he'd left for his girlfriend.

You're the only one who can calm the lightning in my soul and help me find peace.

That last remark he'd made confirmed he'd lost all faith in ever experiencing such an elusive concept again, and once more her foolish heart ached. Not just for Seth but for herself, too. No one could know the emotional wreckage that was left behind when faced with the loss of the person you loved…the hopelessness that ensued. A person had to experience it for themselves before they could even begin to understand.

* * *

It was blissfully quiet and oddly comforting as Seth sat in front of the wood burner, sipping brandy in Imogen's simple front room.

Ahead of his return to the UK he had booked a suite at a five-star hotel, where he might rest and relax and mull over what he was going to do with the Siddonses' house. He still hadn't decided whether he actually wanted to *live* in it. All he'd known when his estate agent friend had rung to tell him that the house was up for sale was that he simply *had* to have it. He didn't really know why, except that it was a significant part of his past and he wanted to right the wrong that had been done there.

But how did you right the wrong of a loved one being taken from the world too soon?

He wouldn't even have the satisfaction of showing James Siddons that he'd exceeded his wealth, thereby proving that he'd kept his word about becoming successful. Who would have believed that a poor car mechanic would become an exceedingly rich dealer in some of the most desirable cars in the world—and friend to the rich and famous on the way?

But even as Seth reflected on what he'd achieved he couldn't deny that underneath it all there was still a sense of something *missing*.

Staring back into the autumn-coloured hues of the burner's flames, he wondered if Imogen had anyone significant in her life. She was a pretty little thing, and kind, too. He was a total stranger to her, but when he'd declared that he needed a drink she'd had no hesitation in offering him some brandy.

He'd been able to tell straight away that she was a

compassionate woman. She was certainly nothing like the majority of well-heeled 'high-maintenance' females he usually came into contact with in New York. Yes, he enjoyed the fact that they flocked round him like bees round a honeypot whenever he was socialising, but lately the ability to attract beautiful and sophisticated women had definitely begun to pall.

Maybe that was also why he'd returned to the UK? Hopefully he could move around unremarked. He didn't have such a glamorous profile here. Except that he might yet have to deal with the curiosity of the media when the citizens of his hometown noted that he'd returned...

The combination of the heat from the fire and the brandy he'd consumed couldn't help but make Seth's eyelids droop. Seconds later he'd fallen asleep, with his head resting against a diamond-patterned cushion he'd placed behind him.

He didn't register Imogen's return. Nor did he see the generous plate of sandwiches she'd brought with her from the kitchen. He'd fallen into the deepest sleep he'd had in years.

When he eventually stirred he couldn't believe the time. Evidenced by the morning light that he glimpsed behind the room's slatted rattan blinds, several hours had elapsed. The cosy fire in the burner had long perished and the room was decidedly chilly, despite the woollen throw that Imogen must have draped over his knees.

It took him aback to realise he must have been asleep for most of the night... How could that be? How could he have let his guard down like that in front of a complete stranger? It just didn't make sense.

Rubbing his hand round his beard-roughened jaw, he pushed the throw aside and sat up. Maintaining the same position for several hours had inevitably cramped his body. A dull ache that bordered on the painful throbbed through his entire being. Rising to his feet, he stretched his arms up high over his head and rolled his shoulders. His mouth was as dry as a sun-bleached riverbed and he was in dire need of water.

Strolling out into the kitchen, he flicked on the light and immediately saw the cling film–wrapped tray of sandwiches on the worktop. Had Imogen made those to share with him last night? Even as Seth had the thought he realised how hungry he was. What an idiot he was for falling asleep like that!

Pouring a glass of water, he gulped down several mouthfuls. His thirst sated, he helped himself to a couple of sandwiches and hungrily wolfed them down. Then he returned to the living room.

He was just rolling up the blinds when his hostess walked in, wearing lavender-coloured pyjamas and a matching dressing gown, her chestnut hair a mass of eye-catching curls. It stopped him in his tracks to notice that her skin was nothing less than flawless...even at this unearthly hour.

'Good morning,' he greeted her huskily.

Her big brown eyes mirrored her astonishment. 'You're still here!'

'I'm afraid I am. You should have woken me and told me to go home.'

Imogen smiled delicately. 'You were sleeping so soundly when I came back from the kitchen I didn't want to disturb you. You were obviously very tired. But shock can do that to a person.'

Seth was puzzled. 'Shock?'

'The note?' she reminded him gently.

Finding himself reacquainted with the letter he'd written to Louisa all those years ago and learning that she'd read it before she died must have been responsible for lowering his defences. He would never normally make himself so vulnerable. Undoubtedly the generous glass of brandy he'd drunk had helped...

CHAPTER THREE

GRAVEL VOICED, SETH COMMENTED, 'It's not every day that your past comes back to haunt you like that.'

Imogen frowned. 'Would you like to keep the note? After all, it really belongs to you.'

He recalled that he'd automatically shoved it down into his coat pocket. 'I'd better hold on to it. I wouldn't want to risk it falling into the wrong hands.'

The brunette's flawless brow crumpled. 'I admit I'd hoped that I could keep it…' Hugging her arms over her chest, she was lost in thought for a moment. 'It's the most romantic thing I've ever read. The words struck a chord. They gave me hope.'

'What I felt for Louisa wasn't romantic. It was just true. I didn't want to *own* her, as though she was some possession. I wanted the very best for her, whatever that was.'

Swallowing down the lump that rose inside his throat, Seth sighed.

'People think that I've mourned her for too long—that missing her is wasted time. Many times I've been told I should move on, find someone else to love. I won't deny that at times I've been tempted. There's been no shortage of takers, wanting me to commit, but so far I haven't been able to do it. Maybe I just loved her too much.'

Shaking his head, he found himself staring at the woman who had given him shelter the night before.

'What did you mean when you said the letter gave you hope?'

'It doesn't matter.'

'But it does. You know my story... Will you tell me yours? Why do you need hope, Imogen?'

'If you think it might help me to talk about things then you're wrong. I'm trying to put what happened behind me and move on. I don't want it to ruin the rest of my life.'

Her expression was peeved, her brown eyes defiant. Seth didn't know why, but he was intrigued. He realised that discussing feelings with a woman might potentially be like walking on broken glass. Whatever angle you came from, it was a delicate issue.

Tunnelling his fingers through his hair, he realised that he really wanted to engage her—to get her to *like* him, even.

'I don't profess to know whether it might help you to talk about things or not—all I'm saying is that if you do decide to I'm willing to listen. What you tell me won't go any further than these four walls... I give you my word.'

Mulling over his remarks, she turned still for a moment. 'And why would you be interested in what happened to me? I'm nothing to you. I'm just some woman who wandered up to your house in the hope that I might find out who wrote the letter I found.'

Seth couldn't help smiling. Did she really not know how attractive she was? The longer he spent in her company, the more he sensed himself becoming attracted to her. He knew that most women wouldn't hesitate to use their physical attributes to their advantage if a man was wealthy or attractive, and he wasn't being falsely modest in realising that he was *both*. The fact that Imogen hadn't made a play for him piqued his interest even more.

'Clearly you're not just "some woman", Imogen. I already sense that you think deeply about things. A lot of men would find that quality very attractive... beguiling, even.'

The unexpected sizzle of desire that suddenly seized him caught him off guard, making him feel distinctly off centre for a minute. Studying her, he saw that even though her dark brown eyes shimmered briefly when she glanced back at him, it was clear Imogen wasn't troubled by the same disconcerting sensations.

Impatient, she moved towards the kitchen. But even as her hand curved round the brass doorknob, she suddenly paused. 'Okay, I'll tell you my story. I owe you that much, since you trusted me with yours. But I'm surprised that you're not in a hurry to go home.'

'I don't have a place here—not unless you count the mansion. For the past ten years I've been living in the States. At the moment home is a hotel suite. Elegant as it is, I'm in no hurry to go back there.'

'You don't have any family that live nearby?'

'My father died when I was a teenager. But, in truth, my mother raised me by herself. My father was far too preoccupied with his drinking and gambling to be of any use to anyone. She's long since moved away from here.'

'What about brothers or sisters?'

'There are none.'

Imogen fell silent again. Then she said, 'I think I'll go and make some tea. Would you like some?'

'I'd prefer coffee...black, no sugar.'

'I'll go and see to it, then. I won't be long.'

'Thanks.'

It wasn't like him actively to *invite* personal conversation, Seth reflected. It must be down to the peculiar intimacy that the dawn had evoked. Just like the night, it could entice a person into letting down their guard and lure them into spilling their innermost secrets... even to a stranger.

What innermost secret was Imogen going to reveal? he wondered.

Splashing his face with cold water and squeezing out some toothpaste to rub round his teeth, he paused to study himself in the bathroom mirror. To his mind, he looked haggard. Seeing the Siddonses' house again had been a real baptism of fire. And he'd gone and *bought* the place! Had he temporarily lost his mind? It was said that love and loss were apt to make people behave strangely...

Rinsing his mouth after using the toothpaste, he registered that he needed a shave. But it wasn't just overnight stubble that darkened his visage.

Even though his path had led him to become seriously wealthy and given him a lifestyle he couldn't have envisaged all those years ago when he'd striven to keep the wolf from the door for himself and his mother, the road had been paved with some gruelling obstacles. If he hadn't made himself impervious to the need for people's good opinion and focused instead on honing his skills and becoming expert at them, he would have been well and truly *lost*.

Even so, living without genuine companionship these past ten years had taken its toll. From time to time basic necessity had driven him to seek out the kind of pleasure that only women could provide, but even great sex didn't come close to true intimacy. The kind of intimacy that he'd shared with Louisa.

His muttered curse vented his frustration.

Having finished his ablutions, he returned to the living room. The enticing aroma of freshly ground coffee filled the air and his stomach growled with hunger.

At some point during Seth's absence Imogen had got dressed. Instead of the pretty lavender pyjamas and dressing gown, she now wore black skinny jeans and a knitted red sweater. Her dark hair was caught up in a hastily arranged topknot, and several loosely curling strands had drifted down over her ears. Her unmade-up complexion was nothing less than translucent, but she visibly coloured pink when she saw that he was silently appraising her.

'All done?' she said quickly.

It was evident that she wanted to deflect his interest. Seth nodded.

'Then I'll just go and use the bathroom myself. I've made your coffee. You'll find it brewing in the kitchen. I've also put some bread into the toaster, if you're hungry. Just help yourself.'

'You must have read my mind. But try not to be too long. We have some talking to do, remember?' Electing not to reply, Imogen hurriedly left. He could already tell that she hadn't appreciated the reminder. Perhaps she wouldn't tell him her story after all?

* * *

Alone again, Imogen was aware that inside her chest her heart was thudding. It was undeniable that she was nervous. But even though the thought of relating to him the recent shattering events she'd endured filled her with something close to dread, she couldn't forget that Seth had shared his own sad story.

Perhaps she should take courage from that? He of all people must understand her reticence about revisiting hurtful events. Just listening to his heartfelt assertion that he would never love anyone as he'd loved the woman he'd lost had been unbearably poignant.

Once upon a time, Imogen had loved Greg with what she'd believed to be similar passionate devotion. However, the idyllic happy-ever-after that she'd hoped for hadn't transpired. Instead, the relationship had come to the most abrupt and devastating end. It would be a very long time—*if ever*—before she trusted another man again...certainly enough to consider sharing her life with him.

'I made some toast for us to share.'

On her return, she saw her handsome visitor's glance was decidedly sheepish. He had filled the silver-plated toast rack with crisped slices of wholemeal bread and brought in the butter dish she'd left on the worktop, along with a pot of marmalade. He hadn't just poured coffee for himself but had made Imogen some tea.

The thoughtful gesture surprised her, and she dropped down into the armchair, taking her beverage with her. 'Thanks. I never would have guessed that you were so domesticated.'

Helping himself to toast and slathering it with a generous portion of marmalade, Seth grinned. The gesture was so distracting it was like the sun bursting through the clouds on a rainy day. She was glad she was sitting down.

'I like to disprove people's assumptions about me,' he drawled: 'It keeps them on their toes.'

Silently sipping her tea, she owned to feeling an odd pleasure at the sight of the businessman enjoying his breakfast. The realisation made her pause. Talking of assumptions—was she *wrong* to think that he was a businessman? Although he dressed like a well-heeled broker in the city of London, the fact that she didn't know what he did made her remember how little she knew about him.

Yet she'd trusted him enough to let him sleep undisturbed on her couch the whole night!

Before she shied away from quizzing him, she asked, 'Do you mind if I ask what you do for a living?'

The wariness that stole across his sublimely carved features indicated his reluctance to answer. It came back to her that when he'd first met her he'd asked if she was a reporter.

'No. I don't mind. I run several motor car dealerships in America.'

'What kind of motor cars?'

'High-end ones... Maserati, Ferrari and Lamborghini to name a few.'

Imogen's stomach lurched helplessly. If she'd needed a reminder that his affluent lifestyle must be about a trillion miles away from hers, then she'd just got one...

'Is there a very big demand for such cars?'

'Hell, yes!' Pausing to gulp down some coffee, Seth wiped the back of his hand across his lips. 'I wouldn't be where I am today if there wasn't.'

He was gazing back at her, and she saw that the blue eyes that were the colour of the most exquisite sapphires glinted disturbingly. But whether it was because her question had irritated him or because he couldn't believe that she was naive enough to ask it, Imogen couldn't tell.

'You mean that you've done well selling them...?'

His ensuing laugh was harsh. 'You think that all I do is to sell cars?'

Her skin crawling with unease, she stared back at him. 'Clearly you're more than just a salesman, but as I don't know very much about the world of fancy cars perhaps you'd enlighten me? I mean...I know you said you ran several dealerships, but—'

'I should have explained. I employ managers to run the dealerships for me. I don't work for the company that sells these cars. I *own* it.'

Talk about having the wind taken out of her sails. With her mouth uncomfortably dry, she took a hasty mouthful of tea. 'Then, it must have been quite a change for you to sleep on my landlord's old couch. I know it's not the most comfortable piece of furniture.'

Frowning, Seth's eyes were doubly piercing as he studied her. 'I was very grateful that you invited me in and allowed me to sleep on it. Did you think I was looking down my nose at you?'

Reaching forward, Imogen stood her cup and saucer on the coffee table. Then she got nervously to her feet. 'I hope you wouldn't be as unkind as that. Look...I'm not trying to rush you, but when you've finished your coffee it's probably best that you go. It's Saturday—my day for catching up with the housework.'

'Haven't you forgotten something?'

Straight away Imogen knew what he meant. Twisting her hands together, she wished she *had* forgotten their agreement. But she immediately saw that Seth Broden *hadn't*. Now on his feet, there was nothing in his expression that told her he might be willing to change his mind.

Before she could talk herself out of it, she blurted out candidly, 'So you really want to know my story, do you? Well, I'll tell you, then...'

Tightly folding her arms across her red sweater, she began.

'I was jilted by my fiancé on our wedding day. Left waiting at the church as if I wore a sign that said Reject on it...'

She paused to take in a breath.

'It was horrendous. I kept trying to ring him, to find out what was going on, but he wasn't taking my calls. And as I sat there, trying to work out what had happened and figure out the reason he wasn't there, the waiting started to feel like the most horrible nightmare that I couldn't wake up from. Time and time again I assured the vicar that he would definitely appear—that perhaps he'd slept through his alarm. But even as I said the words I knew I was only deluding myself. In those interminable few minutes, I went to hell and back. Then I began to do my own private autopsy... I *had* to. Had I missed something in the lead-up to the wedding that should have told me he wanted out?'

She looked forlorn for a second.

'We'd talked about our plans so much. We'd even put a deposit down on a house. We were so excited that we were going to be together at last, in our own home. Greg seemed so happy... I never saw any signs that he wasn't. But apparently he'd been having doubts about us for months. He said that the time just never seemed right to tell me—that he didn't want to hurt me.

'But it wasn't just that. On the day we were due to marry he didn't show up because he was with another woman. Someone from his work he'd been having an affair with. He'd been telling me a bunch of lies all along. I know you probably think I was an utter fool for trusting him, and I agree with you. But I never guessed for so much as a second that he'd rather be with someone else.

'With hindsight I can see that I blinded myself to the truth because I loved him. I told myself that if we had any problems we could surely work them out. To cut a long story short, I believed he was at least honourable. Sadly, it turned out not to be the case. I found out that it's not always an asset to try to see the best in people.'

Quietly, Seth asked, 'How did you find out that he'd been cheating on you?'

'His best man eventually turned up to put me in the picture. To give him credit, it was just as excruciating for him as it was for me. Greg didn't tell him that he'd changed his mind until they met up supposedly to travel to the church.'

Not commenting right away, Seth felt his insides churn with dismay. What a *bastard* to behave so despicably to a sweet girl like Imogen, he thought.

Staring at her, he saw that her huge brown eyes were glassy with tears. Feeling an uncharacteristic urge to dispense comfort, he moved round the table to go to her. Almost immediately she backed away, like a wounded animal when it wanted to lick its wounds in private. Returning to her armchair, she hugged her arms over her chest as though desperately trying to compose herself. Seth stayed where he was.

'What happened to the deposit you paid on the house? Clearly you didn't go through with the purchase if you're renting this place?'

As if in a daze, Imogen glanced up. 'No. I didn't buy it. Greg did. He bought the house with his new girlfriend.'

'*What?* I hope he returned your share of the deposit?'

'As a matter of fact, he didn't. As well as not being honourable, it turned out that he was unscrupulous, as well. He argued that I'd given it to him as a gift. At the moment I'm contesting the case through the law firm I work for. Anyway, that's enough of that. The main thing is that I learned a very hard lesson…one I'm determined not to repeat.'

His appetite for food now gone, Seth thought that it wasn't any wonder that Imogen needed hope. She'd fallen for a man who'd utterly destroyed her trust. Giving your heart to someone was the most trusting thing you could *ever* do, in his opinion. That was why he believed he wouldn't easily give his to a woman again.

'Does your lawyer think you'll win the case?'

The liquid brown gaze held his for a moment and he saw how the little hope that she could muster vied with her underlying fear that she would lose. That made him angry. It made him angry for all the times *he* had lost out to people who'd had more power than him because they'd gone to the right schools or had more money… They had not even thought him worthy of their regard.

He couldn't help but let James Siddons come to mind…

He knew how it felt to be rejected—and something deep inside him didn't want this woman to feel the same.

'My lawyer tells me we won't go down without a fight—but you know what?'

Imogen's smile was uncertain. The vulnerability he detected somehow got to him…made his insides ache.

'What?'

'I don't want to fight. I'd rather keep my energy to rebuild my life. No amount of money is worth getting ill over.'

'If it means the difference between you having the means to make a new start and beginning again with *nothing* I know which one I'd choose.'

'I'll find a way. At least the circumstances I grew up in taught me to be resilient.'

'And what were those?'

'They weren't dissimilar to yours. I was raised by my mum. My dad walked out on her when she fell pregnant with me. He broke her heart, but she never thought for one second that she should give me up. She singlehandedly raised me, working two jobs to keep us together.'

'And where is she now? Does she live close by?'

'No. She eventually remarried and went to live in Spain with her new husband. He's a good man and I'm glad she's with him. She waited a long time to be happy.'

'But that can't have been easy for *you*?'

'No, it wasn't. I did miss her when she left. She agonised about going at all, but when she heard that me and Greg were getting married she felt reassured that I'd be all right. Shame he went and ruined things.'

So not only had Imogen's slimy fiancé abandoned her, but her once devoted mother had, too—albeit for a good reason. It wasn't hard to see that she'd had a tough deal where relationships were concerned. She had good cause to be wary...

'Was she there when he left you high and dry at the wedding?'

Swallowing hard, she looked immediately uneasy. 'She was, but she and her husband were booked on an early-morning flight the next day, so we didn't have a lot of time to talk things over. I was glad that she was there to help explain things to the guests and tell them that there wouldn't be any celebrations. She also helped me cancel the party at the church hall and tidy up. She and my stepfather sat up half the night, offering me consolation, but in the morning he was eager to take her home. I don't blame him. My mum has had enough disappointment in her life without dealing with any more.'

'What about you, Imogen? It must have been tough to deal with your own hurt and disappointment when she left.'

She grimaced. 'I managed. I told you—I'm resilient.'

The morning light that stole through the blinds was getting brighter, and suddenly Seth realised that she ought to have her space back. It wasn't easy to open up to someone and explain such a devastating situation—especially someone you'd only met just a few short hours ago. The funny thing was, he didn't feel as though they were strangers anymore...

Mentally shaking himself, he quickly brought himself back to the present. 'I think I should make myself scarce. I've already taken up way too much of your time. Can I get my coat?'

'Of course.' Startled, Imogen stood up and went outside.

In a matter of seconds she was back with him, the garment he'd asked for still pristine from being hung carefully on the coat stand.

He slipped it on. 'Thanks. It's been good meeting you, Imogen.'

'You, too.'

Her expression suddenly looked shy as he leaned forward to brush her cheek with his lips and he discovered that her translucent complexion was even softer than it appeared. The thought disturbed him more than it should.

He was still thinking about her when he got into his car and drove back to the hotel...

CHAPTER FOUR

IT HAD BEEN a strange few hours. Seth couldn't have predicted the uncanny events that had unfolded on his arrival back in England. He had spent a long and fruitful decade away and, whilst he'd known it would take some degree of adjustment to acclimatise, nothing could have prepared him for what had happened.

To be presented with that heartfelt letter he'd written to Louisa all those years ago at the height of their ill-fated romance had really shaken him up. To have it delivered by a beautiful young stranger who was curious about the writer just because she longed to know how things had worked out had been stranger still.

That afternoon he rang his PA in New York, needing to anchor himself with the familiar.

Returning to his country of birth had made him feel a little off-kilter. And the memory of his encounter with Imogen Hayes inexplicably clung to him. Somehow he couldn't seem to stop thinking about her.

Trusting that he wasn't a threat, she'd allowed him to spend the night on her landlord's couch rather than wake him up when he'd fallen asleep. In his world, kindness like hers was a rarity—if it even existed at all. Nobody did anything without hoping to make some kind of gain. But in his opinion the pretty brunette was far too innocent in the ways of the world—dangerously so—which was probably why she'd fallen prey to a louse like her ex-fiancé.

What he'd give for just five minutes with the man. He'd soon set him straight.

Morgan, the dependable PA who'd worked for him for the past five years in New York, answered her phone. When the preliminary enquiries about how he was doing and the usual niceties were over she relayed his messages. There was one that stood out above all the rest. It was from his old friend Ashraf Nassar— commonly called Ash.

Seth hadn't spoken to him in a very long time but they had been friends since he had met him at a corporate do one night and they'd hit it off. In some ways he'd been Seth's guide and mentor when it had come to negotiating the highs and lows of the city's financial world. Anything a person needed to know about money Ash knew it *all*, it seemed.

He'd been born into Arabian royalty—his father was the ruler of a substantial and powerful kingdom and he was his only son and heir—and he'd had to fight for his freedom to go to New York and utilise his financial knowledge to make a fortune working on Wall Street, knowing all the while that if he failed he had a kingdom waiting for him to oversee when his father died.

Seth called him back immediately.

'Seth! I am *so* glad you rang. Your secretary tells me you've decamped back to the UK? What are you doing there, man?'

Smiling a little ironically to himself—he had yet to fully come to terms with the move himself—Seth told him, 'I'm here because I needed a change. And I've bought a house. A rather grand house. I'm still not quite sure what to do with it...'

Ash chuckled. 'Well, I'm sure that your wife knows what to do with it! I take it you *are* married after all this time, my friend? If not, I demand to know the reason why.'

The question was sobering, to say the least. 'Well, I'm not married, and the reason is I haven't yet found anyone I care for.'

'That is easily remedied. Have an arranged marriage. A beautiful woman who you can tolerate spending a little time with now and again and who will be proud to bear your name and your children for the privilege of being the consort of an important and wealthy man like yourself.'

Frowning, Seth commented, 'Arranged marriages are not really the done thing here.'

'Replace the term with "marriage of convenience", then—something that suits both parties and bypasses the complications of romance. Talking of which...my father is looking for a new supplier of classic sports cars and I recommended you to him. That's why I wanted to get in touch with you. He's very particular when it comes to tradition and marriage—he likes to know that his business partners have settled down and proved themselves when it comes to marriage. If you are to be accepted by the elite classic-car fraternity in his country, you'll need to have a wife. Even a trophy wife would be better than no wife at all. It could be an incredible opportunity for you, Seth.'

It wasn't the suggestion of having a marriage of convenience that stuck with Seth long after his conversation with Ash had ended. It was the phrase 'if you are to be accepted' that lingered. It was the one thing he had striven for in his life and never truly achieved, no matter how much money he made or how much success he had.

But Ash was right. It *was* an incredible opportunity. And didn't he pride himself on making even the most tenuous opportunities work in his favour?

He found himself heading back to the grandiose edifice known as Evergreen to have a proper look round the property. The cheerful name was apt to lead people astray about its presently austere interior, but in the welcome sunlight that streaked through the windows the cavernous rooms seemed far less daunting, less prone to be haunted than they had the day before.

With its voluminous green acres, as well as the generous-size accommodation, there was no doubt that if renovated it might potentially be a terrific place to raise a family...

Lulled into what was almost a pleasant daydream, Seth could hardly believe the thoughts that were tumbling through his brain. He didn't often think about marrying and having a family, even when goaded by his colleagues. The truth was he doubted he had it in him anymore to make such a commitment. Not since Louisa had he seriously entertained the idea—and that had been during a time when he'd had the optimism of youth and dared to believe that anything was possible.

His belittling encounter with her father had changed all that. As well as injuring his pride, it had opened up the old wounds of his childhood, when he'd been yelled at more times than he cared to remember, told that he was useless by his own drunken father. Thank God the man hadn't hung around for long. But being told that you were worthless by someone the rest of the world seemed to look up to—like Siddons—was apt to scar even the strongest of men. No matter *how* determined he was to rise above it.

Yet standing there alone in that remarkable old house, it came to him that he shouldn't deny himself the hope that things could change for the better. His friend Ash had planted a seed with his surprising suggestion. He wasn't searching for love anymore, but what was to stop him from sharing his life with someone and having some kind of helpful connection?

No one wanted to be alone forever—no matter how much money they had. Expensive acquisitions, the admiration of his peers, any amount of pleasure he could buy himself hardly compensated for a lonely old age. Life had to have more meaning than that empty scenario.

He turned to leave the stunning library that had once been filled with books but whose wall-to-wall oak shelves now lay bare, and glanced back over his shoulder at the lush green vista outside the stained-glass windows. It was an exceptionally beautiful view. As he contemplated the scene he went still. Unbidden, an image of Imogen Hayes with her curling chestnut hair, pretty mouth and glossy brown eyes stole into his mind…

It was hard for Imogen to set aside the memory of yesterday and her meeting with Seth Broden. The last thing she could have anticipated was that the man would spend the night on her couch!

The arresting fragrance of his expensive cologne

lingered in the flat long after he had left and it taunted her. She even found herself pressing her face against the cushion he had lain against last night to breathe it in.

Realising what she was doing, she exclaimed, 'Oh, for goodness' sake—what on earth is wrong with me?'

If she was honest, she knew it was the letter he'd sent to his sweetheart that had got to her. It was hard to stop thinking about it. The words had been so tender, so full of love—how could she be anything but entranced by them? Especially when her own experience of falling in love had all but ripped her heart from her chest after her fiancé had waited until their wedding day to demonstrate that he didn't love her at all...that he actually preferred someone else.

The cruel event had happened well over a year ago now, but the pain of it still had the power to wound her afresh whenever it crept up on her unawares. One thing was for certain: she would never make herself so vulnerable to a man again. Her guard would be well and truly up if anyone showed so much as a smidgeon of interest in her.

But as soon as she had that thought the recollection of Seth Broden's lips brushing her cheek as he said goodbye made her grow worryingly warm.

A man like him was way beyond her league, she told herself, and it was pointless to fantasise about him. But there couldn't be many men in the world capable of loving someone so much that when they died they knew they would never love anyone else as deeply again. He was a real one-off.

Sighing, and seeking a diversion, she moved into the kitchen to collect the vacuum cleaner. Then she drowned out her restless and ultimately pointless think-ing with a frenzied bout of vacuuming. When she was done she sat down with a cup of tea and the local paper to search through the small ads for kittens for sale.

Imogen might not expect to have another man in her life but there was nothing stopping her from having a pet as a companion, was there? She didn't know why she hadn't thought of it before.

The loud banging on the front door that evening, when she had just settled down to watch the period drama she'd been following, immediately annoyed her. Pressing the pause button on the remote, she made a half-hearted attempt to tidy her newly washed hair, then went to see who had the audacity to interrupt her programme.

She guessed it might be Rowan, the scatterbrained nurse who lived in the upstairs apartment. She was always forgetting to take her key with her when she left the house.

She'd guessed wrong. The culprit was none other than an impeccably suited, clean-shaven, delicious-smelling and *smiling* Seth Broden. Dumbfounded, Imo-gen stared.

Bypassing the usual niceties, he said casually, 'How long has your bell not been working?'

Wrapping her arms round herself in the black V-neck jumper she wore with jeans, she answered au-tomatically. 'For about two weeks now. I suppose I should really put a note on the door...'

'If it's not just a question of a new battery, then I would get your landlord to fix it.'

She sensed herself blush profusely as he stated the obvious. She blushed even more when she felt one side of her thin jumper slip down over her shoulder. Quickly yanking it back, she said, 'It's not the battery. I checked that. I did ring to ask him to come and sort it out, but his wife told me he was in bed with the flu.'

Seth frowned. 'And you believed that, did you?'

'Why shouldn't I?'

'Because I've learned that you're far too trusting for your own good. That's why. What are you doing this evening? If you've got company I'll turn around and leave. If not, then can I come in?'

Again Imogen stared. She could hardly believe that a man as handsome and rich as Seth Broden would even entertain asking her such a question. It couldn't possibly be because he was interested in her as a woman...could it?

Curling some silken strands of hair round her ear, she shrugged. 'I haven't got company. I was just watching some television. You can come in if you like.'

'I *would* like.' He followed her into the living room and quirked a smile when he saw what was freeze-framed on the television. 'You like that kind of thing, do you? I mean, swashbuckling dramas with plenty of sword-fighting and damsels in distress?'

'I do. It's pure escapism, but that's no bad thing now and again.'

'I agree.' The magnetic blue eyes glinted. 'We all feel like escaping the world from time to time. Although the world *does* have some very agreeable distractions...'

'Like what, for instance?'

'Most things Italian.'

Intrigued, Imogen couldn't resist asking, 'Really? What do you like so much about Italy?'

'For starters, the art, the music—and of course the cars.'

'When you say music, do you mean the opera?'

'Yes.'

'I love it, too. Even though I don't understand the words, the music speaks to me. How could it not? It's so *passionate*.'

She hadn't meant to tell her visitor something as personal as that. She hadn't even shared that particular passion with her friends. They were all big fans of current music and would probably tease the life out of her if she told them she enjoyed listening to opera.

Seth had gone very quiet. He studied her with all the intensity of a scientist on the potential discovery of a vital new specimen. His expression was indisputably fascinated.

To break a silence that had suddenly become uncomfortable, Imogen nervously interjected, 'I didn't expect to see you again so soon—if at all. Is there any particular reason you've called round?'

Breathing out an audible sigh, he replied, 'Yes, there is. Something came to my mind that I want to talk to you about. Oh, and I'd like to invite you out to dinner tomorrow night.'

He might just as well have invited her to NASA in order to fly to the moon with him. Imogen could hardly think straight over her racing heartbeat. And what did he want to talk to her about?

The natural caution that had grown ever stronger after the debacle with her ex was never far away. 'Why do you want to talk to me? You hardly know me. I wouldn't have thought that someone like you would—'

'What do you mean "someone like me"?' His husky

bass voice was both amused and vaguely mocking. 'Do you mean someone that lives and works in a very different world from the one you do, Imogen?'

Grimacing, she once again rearranged the slipping neckline of her sweater more securely over her shoulder. 'Yes, that's exactly what I mean. I'm sure you could talk to any woman you wanted to, with your credentials. It hardly makes sense that you'd want to spend any time with *me*. I'm just an ordinary secretary, Seth. I don't understand your world. I'd be hard pushed to even describe what a Lamborghini looks like, let alone have the opportunity to ride in one!'

'If you harbour such a desire, that could soon be remedied.'

The smile Seth gave her was melt-in-the-mouth irresistible. It had the same delicious effect as sitting in front of a crackling coal fire on a frosty winter's day. It warmed her all over.

'I *don't* have any such desire,' she snapped, feeling testy because she'd been caught off guard. 'You see how different we are? I don't even have a car!'

The faint lines in his otherwise smooth brow crinkled. 'Why don't you have one?'

'I sold it to get a little extra money to pay some bills. That's why I walked to Evergreen yesterday. Not that I mind walking.' Suddenly wary of having his too interested regard, she started to move towards the kitchen. 'Would you like some coffee?'

'Are you saying that you'll agree to talk?'

She should say no, she told herself. If she did, then that would probably be the end of it. But, as though swept away by an unexpected tide she didn't have a hope of fighting, she found herself agreeing. 'I don't suppose it can do any harm...'

'It won't. I'm hoping that what I'm about to discuss might be of benefit to us both. And yes, I think I will have that coffee.'

Waiting for Imogen to return from making their drinks seemed interminable. As Seth sat on the sofa, resting his elbows against his thighs, he attested to having a serious amount of butterflies in his stomach. It wasn't something that happened to him very often—*if* at all. But the step he was considering taking was momentous. It would change the way he lived his life completely if it came to fruition.

Yet he had two very good reasons for contemplating it. The first was his friend's suggestion. It would open many doors for him. And the second was more personally fortuitous. He wanted to live his life differently. And the basis of that desire was the need to share his life with someone—to have a proper connection with another human being that would ensure he didn't grow old and embittered because of the heart-rending loss he'd endured in his early life.

'Here we are.'

Carrying a round wooden tray with their drinks on, Imogen briefly stooped down to the coffee table to arrange the crockery. As she did so the recalcitrant neckline that was proving near impossible to keep in its position glided provocatively down over her shoulder. Not only did Seth get an even closer glimpse of her translucent bare skin, he also caught sight of her arresting cleavage encased in an ebony lace bra.

The sight couldn't help but stir his blood. Loosening his tie a little, he watched her hastily straighten up and knew that she'd caught him studying her... How refreshing to find a woman who blushed so naturally, who didn't use it as an artifice to come on to him, he thought.

'Thanks.' He smiled.

'I made some chocolate cookies earlier. Would you like to try one?'

Before he could reply, Imogen had disappeared into the kitchen again. Seth likened her to a mini whirlwind and the observation made him smile.

When she sat down again a delicious waft of engagingly sweet perfume briefly enveloped him and made his insides clench. She pushed a small plate of mouthwatering biscuits towards him and, already caught in the spell of her femininity, he couldn't resist sampling one.

The sublime taste that filled his mouth immediately elicited his appreciation. 'Mmm. These are terrific. You didn't tell me what a witch you were at baking. Got any other temptations I should know about?'

Raising her cup of coffee, Imogen temporarily shielded her expression from his glance. Intuiting that his last comment had rattled her, Seth could hardly believe the woman could be so innocent. Most women would have taken it as an invitation to at the very least flirt a little...

'I don't bake to try to tempt people. I do it because I enjoy it. If you want to take a couple with you, go ahead.'

'Maybe I will.' His candid gaze leisurely roamed her face. What man *wouldn't* enjoy staring into those big brown eyes? 'Are you ready to have that talk now?'

'I suppose so. What's on your mind?'

'Well...'

Holding the hot mug of coffee firmly between his hands, he took his time thinking how best to phrase his proposition. He had no idea how Imogen would receive the suggestion. She might immediately tell him to leave for all he knew, but he hoped she wouldn't...

'I've been reflecting on our situations. It came to me that we've both been badly hurt in the past, and understandably neither of us wants to entertain the idea of another relationship—at least not one where we put our hearts on the line. I don't know about you, but I don't want to spend the rest of my life alone. I'd like a companion, if nothing else—someone I can share my life with but who wouldn't be beholden to me emotionally. Such an undertaking would also help me in my business dealings. People immediately view men like me as more trustworthy and honourable if they are married. To cut to the chase, I'm asking you if you'd consider being that person, Imogen.'

The atmosphere had suddenly grown tense, as if an impending storm was on its way. Seth honestly couldn't remember the last time he'd experienced being so unsettled.

Shifting in her chair, Imogen took her time answering him. Just when he'd convinced himself she was going to refuse, one corner of her pretty mouth lifted in an amused smile.

'It's funny, but I was thinking about getting myself a companion earlier. I decided that I would get a kitten.'

He frowned. 'A kitten? Is that really all you want to share your life with?'

'It would undoubtedly be a lot less demanding than a man.'

'But it would hardly help support you, would it?'

'I don't want anyone to support me. In any case, I'm hardly going to trust a *man* to help me, am I? I certainly wouldn't risk giving up my independence to one.'

'I don't blame you for feeling that way, but I'm not the idiot who didn't show up on your wedding day, Imogen. If I give my word I *keep* it. I'm a very wealthy man, and if you agreed to my proposition I'd take care of everything financially. You'd never have to worry about where you were going to live or how you were going to manage again. It goes without saying that I would give you a generous allowance.'

Taking a deep breath in, Seth breathed out and studied the brunette. So far he couldn't gauge what she was feeling. There was no longer any suggestion of a smile. Instead, her expression was carefully guarded. He decided to carry on.

'In return...I'd like you to come and live with me. That would mean that whenever I travelled abroad for work, or simply when I wanted a vacation, you would go with me as my companion. It wouldn't mean you couldn't do other things. I like to think that I'm a reasonable man. But I would never tolerate you bringing my name into disrepute. It's not too onerous, but I have a somewhat public profile because of what I do, and I've already entrusted some very personal information to you. I wouldn't want to risk my story being sold to the newspapers. It goes without saying that I would never reveal what you've told me to anyone else. What we've shared is just between the two of us and private. To sum up—if you're in agreement, I'd like to make our arrangement official.'

Seth saw the colour in her face drain a little.

'What do you mean, exactly?'

'I'm suggesting that we do things legally and get married.'

CHAPTER FIVE

IMOGEN WAS STUNNED. So stunned that she couldn't *think*, let alone speak. In a bid to engage her brain with her mouth, she gulped down some coffee. When she glanced up and saw that Seth's blisteringly blue eyes were all but eating her up as he waited for her answer, she murmured, 'You're serious?'

'Yes, I am. I don't have time to play games, Imogen. I've been on my own for a long time. It wouldn't be a one-sided arrangement. As I told you before, it would benefit us both.'

'And how do you work that out? Isn't your work mainly in the States? I live and work *here*, Seth.'

'I'm opening a new dealership in London, so it's very likely I'll be based here for a while. If I have Evergreen renovated and refurbished we could live there. In the meantime I'm going to look for another house for us to move into,'

'Slow down a bit. I haven't agreed to anything yet. My head's reeling!'

Her companion sighed and scraped back his hair. 'I realise that my suggestion must have come as quite a surprise, but I believe it's a good one. It makes sense for us to get together and help each other out.'

'I'm not as sure about that as you seem to be, Seth. What about my job? If I were to accept your offer, what would I do about that?'

His scorching blue gaze never left hers. 'To start with I'd like you to give a month's notice with the proviso that you'll be available to me should I need you.'

'And what am I supposed to tell my boss?'

'You can tell her that you're going to be married and that your new husband wants you to help him run his business.'

'But you *don't* want me to work for your business, do you? You want to hire me as a paid companion.'

A muscle flinched at the side of Seth's jaw. He wasn't finding it easy to hide his impatience. 'I want you to become my wife. That's all your boss needs to know.'

'Don't you think the news is going to come as a bit of a shock? Especially as she knows I haven't been seeing anyone and that I vowed I wouldn't for a very long time?'

'You can tell her it all happened very quickly.'

Colouring at the thought of her and Seth having an immediate undeniable attraction to each other that would only be satisfied by them living together as man and wife, Imogen shook her head. 'I doubt if she'll believe that. And don't forget I'm still dealing with a court case to try to get my deposit back from my ex.'

'Let me speak to her about that. I'll pay any costs that are outstanding and cover the deposit myself. You've already told me that you don't need the stress of getting into a fight with your ex for it, and nor do you need to. He's old news—*gone*. Erase him from your mind. From now on I'll be looking after you.'

Despite her lack of trust that such a premise was

at all likely, the declaration was irresistibly seductive. What woman *wouldn't* want a man like him to take care of her? Imogen mused. But her surprise at his words mingled with not a little annoyance as she contemplated his steely-eyed glance.

'You make it sound so straightforward and it isn't. I don't *need* you to look after me. I'm not a helpless little girl. I'm sure you mean well, but agreeing to have a relationship—*any* relationship as far as I'm concerned—is crazy. Is it likely that I'd want to risk walking into something that's potentially going to hurt me again?'

Getting to his feet, Seth stared down at her. 'If you don't involve your emotions...and I personally don't intend to...you *won't* get hurt. As for getting to know each other—I'm sure that will happen given time.'

If he knew what she was thinking right then—that it wasn't much of a deal to get married to someone who took care of the practicalities of the relationship but didn't engage his feelings—she wondered if he would understand. Even though she'd been terribly hurt—her heart broken and her self-esteem in tatters after what her ex had done—deep down inside Imogen still hadn't given up on the idea of a truly loving union with a man.

'That may be so, and I'm sure there are many women who would be only too happy to be the companion of a wealthy man like you, and have everything they need taken care of. But that's not me. I need to make a contribution in life—not just be a taker. So all I can say is thanks for considering me, but I'm afraid I'm going to have to refuse.'

For a moment Seth's charismatic features radiated shocked surprise. Then, breathing out an impatient sigh, he said. 'You wouldn't just be *taking* from me, Imogen. Your concern is commendable, and it reassures me that my decision is the right one. I fully expect you to do your fair share, if you undertake to commit to this partnership, and I want to emphasise that you wouldn't be walking completely into the unknown. For instance there's plenty of information about me on the internet, if you want to investigate. My profile is there for all to see. I've got nothing to hide.'

'That may be so, but you don't find out the truth about someone until you spend time with them. What can facts on the internet tell me about the *real* Seth Broden?' Imogen was adamant that social media wasn't to be relied upon, even though she had straight away detected that Seth didn't like her doubting him. 'For instance, can it tell me what your values are, or if you're a man that can be trusted?'

'You trusted me enough to let me spend the night on your couch and you didn't come to any harm. If you're willing to get to know me better you'll discover that honesty is important to me in *all* my dealings. I trust that my behaviour towards you will help illustrate that.'

Sighing, she brushed her hair back from her cheek. 'It's not that I don't want to get to know you. What I've learned about you so far pleases me. The letter that you wrote to Louisa makes me know intuitively that you're a good man...a sincere one. But I wouldn't want to promise you something I couldn't deliver. Honesty is important to me, too. What if I changed my mind after we got married and decided that I'd made a mistake?'

'I won't pretend I wouldn't be disappointed. But neither would I coerce you into staying. If you were really intent on ending things I'd have to respect that.

I'd also ensure that I set you up with the means to start your life over again somewhere else. For instance if you wanted to start up a business for yourself or study for a new career I'd do everything in my power to help you. I can't say fairer than that. Still...' He paused to survey her. 'I'd expect you to enter into our initial agreement in the spirit of genuinely trying to make it work. Do you agree?'

Although she didn't *want* to deny that in truth she yearned for much more than that—that she wanted to hold out for the truly loving union with a man that had always been her dream—Imogen saw that she'd have to suppress those feelings if she was going to go through with this marriage. To forgo the loving relationship she longed for was the last thing she wanted to do—the very thought was like a splinter in her heart—but at least Seth was promising that he'd compensate her if their partnership didn't work out. If he kept his promise it would give her a lot more options about what she did in the future, even if it was destined to be a lonely one.

She told him, 'Yes. If I were to accept going into this arrangement you're proposing, I promise you I'd endeavour to make it a successful one. But you know women *do* change their minds sometimes? I mean, if you started something that turned out to be wrong would *you* stick with it?'

The comment elicited a surprising smile.

'I don't expect you to do any such thing. But don't you have to give something a chance before you decide it's not working? In any case, why *shouldn't* our partnership work out? We both need human contact, and what I want in my life is a warm, sentient woman. Someone I can talk to—someone who's willing to listen to my problems when I have them and offer her opinion…as I will do for you. I want someone who'll be there if I need to take a partner to a business function or go out to dinner, someone who's intelligent and pretty, with a softness that reminds me not to get too cynical about life. I want someone like *you*, Imogen.'

Before she had time to process this statement, Seth reached down and wrapped his hand round hers. The touch of his flesh was dizzying. Then he gently but firmly pulled her to her feet.

'I'm offering you a once-in-a-lifetime opportunity. Do you want to let it pass you by and regret it for years to come?'

'I've had my fair share of regret, without adding any more to the list. But if I was to do this I'd need to do something useful to earn my keep besides just being there for you.'

He was still holding on to her hand, and the touch of his firm, warm skin was indisputably battering down her defences.

His response to her remark was sure and unhesitant.

'Make no mistake. You'll have plenty to keep yourself occupied. Living with me is going to open up a very different lifestyle to the one you've been used to and you'll have to adapt to it. It's a world where money is no object…where people literally spend *millions* on houses, cars and haute couture. It's a completely different world. For instance, when you travel with me on business you're going to have to be able to converse with some very influential men and women as we socialise. As my wife, you're going to have to reflect everything I stand for and act accordingly.'

Imogen immediately started to disengage herself

from his hand. Whilst the prospect of learning to live in the kind of world he described might be an amazing opportunity, and one that would undoubtedly help take her mind off her past disappointments and sorrows, it also frightened her right down to her bones.

She started to shake her head. 'I don't think I could do it, Seth. You'd best find someone else.'

'Why? Are you telling me that you never want to be challenged? Do you always want to stay safe and predictable?'

The remark stung. 'That's not fair. You're asking me to make a momentous change to my life. You've heard what I've been through. Surely you can understand why I'm unsure?'

His lips split into a smile that was nothing less than dazzling. 'It's okay to be unsure. It's only human. But to let that stop you taking a risk is just plain foolish.'

'I know I've made some bad decisions, but that doesn't mean I'm foolish. I've given my trust too easily, that's all.'

'You haven't trusted *yourself*—that's why. You think that other people know better, and of course that's not true. You need to see that you're equally capable of making good decisions.'

'I'm sure you're right. But I need some more time before I answer your proposition. Will you give me that?'

'How much more time?'

'I—I don't know…' She knew her uncertainty must show on her face, but Seth wasn't going to let that stop him from pressing home his point.

'How about telling me tomorrow?' he said. 'I'd

planned to take you out to dinner anyway. We'll go somewhere classy and intimate.'

'I'd rather talk in private rather than having our conversation somewhere public.'

Narrowing his gaze, he fired an out-of-the-blue volley with a melting grin that was just about the sexiest thing she'd ever witnessed. He might as well have poured gasoline into her blood and set it on fire, Imogen thought.

'In truth, so would I, beautiful. I'll come here, then. We'll postpone dinner and just talk. What time shall I call round?'

'If you can drop by tomorrow afternoon I'll let you have my decision then.'

Lightly shaking his head with a rueful smile, Seth moved towards the door. 'I'll be on tenterhooks till then. You can count on it. Expect me around one, then.'

Suddenly dismayed, in case her request had driven him away for good, Imogen clutched at her belly. 'You're leaving…just like that?'

'The sooner I leave, the sooner you'll have time to think things over. I've already indicated to you that it won't be easy for me to wait. Anyway, I think it's time we said good-night, don't you?'

Imogen hardly registered the fact that Seth had moved towards her, he'd moved so stealthily. However, she most definitely registered the warm and seductive touch of his lips as they brushed against her cheek just before he turned round and left…

Seth spent the most horrendous night, unable to sleep. Even as he scanned through the internet or watched television as a means of distraction he knew nothing would still his disquiet and impatience that Imogen hadn't immediately accepted his offer of marriage.

He owned that it had hurt his pride. It was no exaggeration that *any* other woman he'd asked to be his wife would have been nothing less than ecstatic at the prospect. But, although he couldn't explain it, he also knew that no other woman interested or beguiled him like Imogen did.

All he could do now was pray that she would see sense and give him the answer he wanted. Surely, in light of everything that had happened to her, she would start to see that Seth's proposal was the only sensible thing that could guarantee her a happier future? After all, he was the one man who could provide virtually anything her heart desired...*wasn't* he?

When he arrived at her flat the next day Imogen looked as though she, too, had had a restless night. Her soft brown hair was slightly disarrayed and there were faint dark circles beneath her eyes. He owned to feeling reassured. Whatever her decision, he saw that she hadn't made it easily. That meant she was taking his proposal seriously—that she was giving it proper consideration.

'All right, Seth,' she began. 'I don't mind telling you I've had the worst night I've had since I was stood up in church on my wedding day.'

He flinched, but quickly recovered. 'I'd like to tell you I'm sorry about that, but that rather depends on your decision.'

Her cheeks searing with heat, she answered, 'Well, to put you out of your misery, I'll tell you.'

'Good.' Aiming for a confident smile, he found he couldn't quite manage it. His nervous anticipation at what she was going to say gripped his gut like a fist. If he'd had a mind to say a prayer just then, he would have offered one up.

Imogen's insides lurched as she glanced up at Seth. His proposal of marriage was even more daunting now that she saw him again in the flesh. When he had left yesterday she'd honestly feared that she might never see him again. If she didn't know better, she'd think that he was becoming important to her...

But how could that be? she asked herself. His proposal wasn't a *real* one, in that it didn't come out of love for her, and she would be cheating herself if she said that didn't matter. It mattered a great deal. She *shouldn't* give up on the idea of finding love and settle instead for a marriage of convenience—no matter how alluring Seth Broden happened to be. Having already been devastatingly taken in by her previous fiancé, she knew she was dicing with danger in even considering his offer...

'Imogen?' Seth prompted.

Clasping her hands, she stole a shuddering breath. 'I've decided to take up the offer of becoming your full-time companion.'

Her mouth dried even as she said the words. The words that would change her life and give her a future she'd never imagined even in the most fanciful of her dreams. The words that would align her to a man she'd only met a couple of days ago—a charismatic stranger with a sorrowful past who had left the country to go and make his fortune.

The success he'd achieved was astounding. But then, Seth Broden obviously walked his talk... He *had* trusted himself and it had paid off. Why couldn't it work for her if she did the same? she mused nervously. After all, right now, what did she have to lose?

'And my wife.'

'And your wife.'

Seth's hypnotic smile vanished as soon as she'd agreed. In its stead, his expression became serious and businesslike. 'Good. Now we can both move forward.'

Trying to sound more confident than she was feeling, Imogen commented, 'Presumably I'll have to give in my notice as soon as possible, as well as give up my tenancy on the flat?'

Even as she spoke she felt even more as though she were in a dream. Suddenly nothing seemed remotely real anymore. She might just as well have been on a raft, drifting out into an endless intimidating ocean with no hope of ever finding land again... That was how scared the prospect of living with Seth made her feel.

He frowned just then, and it drew her attention to his smooth forehead and his exquisitely carved cheekbones. A frisson of excitement replaced her fear as she reminded herself that she had just agreed to marry him.

'Yes, you will,' he confirmed. 'But you'll be going on to something better on both counts. Don't forget that. I can have the necessary agreements drawn up by my lawyer in the morning, stating clearly what you will be committing to. Then you can have it legally verified. After that, the marriage can be arranged. Can you let me have some ID?'

Feeling a bit like a lamb startled by a wolf, Imogen felt her heart skitter wildly. 'Give me a few minutes and I'll get what you need.'

She headed off to the bedroom, where she kept her personal files. When she returned and handed him the necessary documents Seth didn't hide his relief. He slipped them into the inside pocket of his flawless silk-lined jacket.

Then, taking up the conversation where they'd left off, he said, 'I'll book dinner at the Dorchester for us tomorrow night. I'll pick you up at around seven to take you to the restaurant, and once we're there we can discuss things in more depth and start to get to know each other. Do you have anything suitable to wear? If you don't, I'll get something delivered to you.'

The inside of Imogen's mouth turned ever drier. She had never worn a really expensive outfit in her life. Outside work, vintage and secondhand clothing was more her thing. And Seth was taking her to the *Dorchester.* It was known to be one of the most revered hotels in the world.

Desperately trying to make sense of it all, she knew her smile was shaky. 'You don't even know what size I am.'

Lifting an amused eyebrow, he let those sapphire-blue eyes matter-of-factly appraise her figure. 'I'm pretty good at making an assessment. Leave it to me.'

'If your choice doesn't work out I can always wear the dress I bought to wear at my wedding reception. It's still hanging untouched in my wardrobe.'

Straight away, she saw that he didn't find the suggestion remotely acceptable—anything *but.*

'I don't think a reminder of what your ex did to you would be a good way of starting our relationship... do you?'

She was immediately chastened. Her skin had heated as though she were sitting beneath a raging sunlamp. 'I was trying to be ironic. Never mind. I'll expect to see you tomorrow at seven.'

'You'll need shoes to go with the outfit. What size do you wear?'

'I'm a five.'

'That's all I need to know for now. In the meantime, I'd like to try to dispel any awkwardness between us now, rather than leave it until later when our plans are underway. Why don't you come over here?'

'Why?'

'Take a risk and find out.'

As if compelled by some otherworldly force, she obliged. When Seth put his hand on her shoulder for a startling couple of seconds she was acquainted with the sensuous touch of his silkily warm flesh against hers. She couldn't suppress a gasp.

'Please forgive the liberty...' he breathed softly, and gently adjusted the material of the same sweater she'd worn yesterday because the shoulder had gone awry again.

Ever since he'd put his proposal to her she'd been dazed—too dazed to think about what to wear—and she had grabbed the first thing that had come to hand this morning. Glancing up at him, she started to say that it wasn't a problem, and immediately tried to engineer some distance between them.

But before she could slip out of his grasp he bent his head towards hers. Startled, Imogen knew that he was going to kiss her... When his mouth gently but firmly touched hers, she learned that even his lips tasted luxurious. Everything about the man was exclusive and expensive, and she was already in way over her head, succumbing to his charm, intensely focused and aware.

Time seemed to thicken and slow down. The thought came to her that if she'd ever wondered what it would be like to be thoroughly seduced by a master of the art she'd just been given a delicious taster…

Even before he kissed Imogen, Seth guessed he would be entranced by the touch of that sultry mouth beneath his and he was *right*. Although he'd been annoyed with her for not accepting his proposal straight away, all was now forgotten because she'd finally said yes.

What was more surprising was that any residual doubts he might have had completely fled as he touched his lips to hers. Now he realised that if they hit it off sexually it couldn't help but make their partnership all the more sweet.

But even as he had the thought his well-honed instinct for survival kicked in. It had long been part of the essential armour that protected him. It didn't matter how much he wanted to trust Imogen, he couldn't afford to let down his guard. He'd be a fool if he did.

Carefully withdrawing his lips, he smiled. He also shouldn't forget that she'd been well and truly taken to the cleaners by her ex-fiancé, and he didn't want her to think that he might be similarly unscrupulous.

'That was nice…' he murmured.

Briefly touching his hand to her incredibly soft cheek, he stepped away. Imogen grimaced. Her unsure expression suggested that she regretted the unexpected intimacy they'd just shared. Her next comment confirmed it.

'I had assumed that this partnership wouldn't involve any intimacy between us…that it would be purely for convenience?'

Seth stared at her. 'All I will say to that, Imogen, is why don't we just wait and see how things unfold? I certainly wouldn't expect you to be intimate with me if you didn't want that, too.'

'I'm glad we're clear about that, then.'

'Good. Now, let me give you my mobile number so you can ring me if you need anything.' He opened his wallet and gave her his business card. 'I'd better go.' Heading towards the door, he glanced over his shoulder, adding, 'If you've never been to the Dorchester before, I know you're going to love it.'

Stepping into the prestigious West End showroom of which he'd just become the new owner, it was once more brought home to Seth why he loved the cars on display so much. Every time he set eyes on a Lamborghini his stomach flipped as if he'd just completed a one-hundred-and-fifty-degree roll in a stunt plane. They weren't just classy. With their sleek lines, flawless bodywork and powerful engines, they oozed excitement. He still thought it a privilege to drive one, let alone to be the owner of *several*.

The manager, a good-looking Italian called Paolo Bellucci, who had flown out to New York to be interviewed by Seth for the post, immediately came over to greet him.

'*Ciao*, Signor Broden. Welcome to your new showroom. I trust you are happy to be home again in the UK?'

They shook hands and Seth affirmed that he was. For the first time since he'd been back on British soil he found that he honestly meant it.

'Can I invite you into the office to enjoy a cup of

real Italian coffee and meet the rest of the staff?' Paolo asked.

Seth was pleased to oblige. Their simple little exchange had made him feel at home. Good customer service had been one of the cornerstones of his success, and he was always pleased to note it from anyone else.

But that wasn't the only thing that made him feel glad. Tonight he would be meeting Imogen to take her out to dinner. And he hadn't forgotten the visit to the exclusive fashion house he'd arranged.

A frisson of pleasure shivered through him as he thought about what kind of dress might complement her charming figure. He'd already decided it would be a dress and not a trouser suit. It would highlight her femininity. But whatever the outfit he chose, he knew that her glossy brown eyes and pretty face would undoubtedly enhance it.

In the plush furnished office, a young assistant was despatched to bring Seth and the new manager their coffee.

When he returned with the beverages, Paolo smiled and said, 'I taught him how to make it myself.'

Freeing the button on his single-breasted pinstriped jacket, Seth sat back in the comfortable leather chair and relaxed. 'Any small touches that make the customer feel important are always an asset,' he remarked.

The other man nodded in agreement. 'If anyone knows how to give the customer what they want, it's you, Signor Broden. Your success in the industry speaks for itself. You epitomise everything about these cars. Frank Sinatra was once quoted as saying, "You buy a Ferrari when you want to *be* somebody.

You buy a Lamborghini when you *are* somebody." It must be very gratifying to know that.'

Seth frowned. Once upon a time such a quote would undoubtedly have stroked his ego, but he was long past the stage when that alone gave him any real satisfaction. He wanted the chance to be accepted into the elite fraternity in Ash's father's kingdom that his friend had talked about, and that was because it felt like a final frontier he had to cross.

To be accepted by a seriously important man like the sheikh would be high honour indeed. Maybe then the incessant desire to prove himself as being as good as anybody else and be accepted would finally start to ease. In the meantime he would concentrate on finding a different sort of satisfaction in something more meaningful. His priorities were starting to change.

As if he intuited what he was thinking, Paolo commented, 'No doubt your wife is also enjoying being back in England?'

Firming his lips, Seth reached for his coffee. 'I'm not married.' Before he tasted the inviting cappuccino, he added, 'But I intend to be very soon.'

'*Complimenti*. Congratulations. Who is the lucky *signorina*?'

'Her name is Imogen. But please don't talk to anyone from the press about it. The lady is somewhat shy, and I'd like to ensure her privacy for as long as I can.'

'But of course.'

A knock at the door heralded the appearance of the rest of the dealership staff, and Seth brought his attention back to the business in hand. But almost unconsciously he regularly consulted the time on his Rolex. He expressly didn't want to be late for his appointment at the fashion house, and nor did he want to get back too late to collect his agreement to marry Imogen from his solicitor…

CHAPTER SIX

'THIS IS FOR YOU. I hope you approve. There are also some shoes that complement the dress. Why don't you go and try them on?'

Effortlessly handsome and imposing, dressed in yet another flawless bespoke suit, Seth stood at her front door. He handed Imogen a chic shiny carrier bag with the name of a famous French designer emblazoned on it.

Accepting it made her nervous. She knew she was acting as though a live grenade was inside that might go off at any second... Even if she worked from dawn until dusk, seven days a week, she wouldn't be able to afford even the simplest outfit from such an exclusive designer.

'Thanks. I'll check it out in a minute,' she said quietly. 'Why don't you come in?'

Once back in her living room, she felt a bit more as if she was on firmer ground.

As Seth shut the door behind him, his glance was quizzical. 'What's wrong?'

'I know you said that you'd get me something to wear, but I didn't expect you to spend this sort of money on it.' Holding the bag aloft, as if to remind him who the designer was, Imogen wasn't surprised when he responded with the most casual of shrugs.

'Don't you like her work?'

She almost spluttered. 'Don't I *like* her work? I know who she is—of course I do. But her designs are well out of my league, Seth. You shouldn't have spent so much. If you have the receipt I'm sure they'll take it back. Just give me a few minutes longer and I can find something else to wear.'

'I don't doubt that you could find something passable and make it look like a million dollars, sweetheart, but the fact is I *want* you to wear this outfit. We're going to be seen out in public together for the first time and, like it or not, people will note *exactly* what you're wearing and where it came from.'

She lowered the bag down by her side as she was reminded that the man she'd agreed to marry was not just wealthy, but famous for his achievements, as well. In a classy hotel like the Dorchester word would quickly get round that Seth Broden had returned to the UK.

She'd seen the most incredible photograph of him on his website. In it he looked so gorgeous that she would defy *any* woman not to want him. He was leaning against the bonnet of a shiny red Lamborghini and the tag line underneath read, 'The car maketh the man…' It didn't even mention his name. Clearly everyone in the exclusive world he moved in knew only too well who he was.

Her teeth worried anxiously at her lip. What was she letting herself in for, and could she handle it?

But she didn't have time to fret about that now. 'Okay. I'll go and try these on. But if they don't fit, or they're uncomfortable, you're going to have to let me wear something of my own.'

Seth smilingly acquiesced. 'Agreed… But I'll bet my bottom dollar that everything will fit perfectly.'

Imogen didn't reply. She got the feeling he was supremely confident that he was right.

She opened the door and went down the hallway to her bedroom. After putting the glossy bag down on the bed, she unpacked the fragrant pink tissue paper that enfolded the garment and murmured softly, 'Oh, my Lord…'

Gently lifting the lawn-green dress that was inside, she silently acknowledged that the flawless silk was to die for. Holding the material against her, she saw that the design was sleeveless and that it fell gracefully to just below the knee. It had a contemporary wrapped waist. She wasn't nearly so confident as Seth was that it would fit her, but she couldn't help praying that it would.

A few minutes later, as she stood in front of the wardrobe mirror, she could hardly believe that the woman she was looking at was *her*. The dress was a perfect fit. More than that, wearing it couldn't help but boost the self-esteem that had been flagging for months now. She had finally discovered what women meant when they said a new outfit made them feel like a million dollars.

Seth had found the perfect colour for her in choosing the lawn green. Not only did the shade complement her natural colouring, the design of the dress indisputably highlighted her femininity. Imogen rarely bought clothing that would do that. Her clothes were usually practical, or quirky in some way, and that was what she stuck to.

And then she tried on the shoes. They were a luxurious black leather court with a gold-coloured kitten heel. They might have been *made* for her.

Allowing herself a small twirl, she smiled at her reflection.

Before she went out to show Seth how she looked she hung back for a few more minutes to retouch her make-up and brush her hair. After touching perfume to her wrists and behind her ears, she collected her favourite black wool coat and returned to the living room.

Dropping the coat onto the arm of a nearby chair, she straightened and looked at Seth. He stared. For a tense moment his jaw briefly clenched and she wondered what he was feeling. He told her.

'You look incredible. You put me in mind of one of those glamorous movie stars from the fifties. Do you realise this is the first glimpse I've had of your legs? I guessed they would be shapely. I'm glad I chose a dress for you.'

Letting down her guard, Imogen didn't hide her pleasure. 'It's wonderful! Even the shoes fit perfectly. I'm sorry if I seemed ungrateful.'

His blue eyes flashed. 'I never thought for a moment that you were being ungrateful. I realise that you just aren't used to feeling that you deserve nice things, better treatment than you've settled for in the past. It's not a crime to enjoy some luxury and to expect decent behaviour from the man in your life. The majority of men would naturally want to treat you as you deserve, Imogen. I don't think I'm unusual.'

It was strange, having him refer to himself as the

man in her life. She was still unsure around him, not quite believing that he would choose *her* to be his wife and companion over anyone else—but having dipped her toe in the water, she had to take a chance and swim...

'Hadn't we better go? I've just noticed the time.'

'You're right. Put on your coat and we'll go out to the car.'

Imogen had another surprise when they went outside and Seth led her to their vehicle. Instead of the comfortable sedan that she'd expected, parked kerbside was a silver-coloured Lamborghini. Up close, its sleek, flawless lines were like nothing she'd ever seen before. It practically demanded that people stopped and stared, whether they loved cars or not.

She caught her breath. 'We're going to London in *this*?'

Seth chuckled in delight, and the compelling sound cascaded through her body like a shower of electrical sparks. She was tingling all over.

'I thought I'd introduce you to another little luxury.' He smiled. 'The manager of my new dealership loaned it to me for the night. I remembered you said that you'd never experienced riding in one, and I thought it the ideal opportunity to show you what it was like.'

Moving round to the passenger door, he opened it. Before she sat down he helped remove her coat, then waited as she lowered herself onto the butter-soft leather seat and closed the door.

It was one of the most exhilarating experiences Imogen had ever had, travelling down the motorway in such an incredible car. But it was even more exhilarating to watch Seth handle the driving. He applied himself to the task with the kind of consummate skill and dexterity only someone extremely experienced could utilise. What must it be like to be as confident as that? she wondered.

Briefly stealing a glance at her, he remarked, 'I'm wondering what you're thinking about.'

'I'm thinking that I can hardly believe I'm doing this… It seems so surreal.'

'But you're enjoying it?'

'Yes, I am. It's made me realise how cautious I've become. I've shied away from doing anything remotely risky in case it backfires on me—even having *fun*. I really want to try to change that.'

'That's good to hear. We're ahead of the game. Maybe enjoying yourself is just what was needed. Taking risks isn't so bad after all, hmm?'

Meeting his gaze, she flushed. Then she glanced away again. Maybe she *had* lowered her expectations for too long. What could be wrong in raising them a little? She might not fulfil her desire of meeting a like-minded soul who wanted a loving long-term relationship as she did, but perhaps being with someone like Seth would provide other things that would compensate. All she could do was wait and see what transpired.

After being shown to their elegantly dressed table beneath the glinting chandeliers of the dining room, Seth and Imogen took their seats. Seth schooled himself to relax. After all, what had he to worry about? Fate had dealt him a very unexpected but fortunate hand.

Not only had he been presented with the fortuitous opportunity to become the sheikh of Ayabador's supplier of classic sports cars, but he hadn't been back at home for very long before it had brought the pretty and delightful Imogen Hayes into his path.

Studying her across the table just then, he mused that she might well turn out to be the perfect companion for him. Although he personally didn't like the term, she would be exactly the 'trophy wife' that his friend Ash had suggested he find.

Not only was she pleasant to be around, but she was young and inexperienced enough to see the necessity of taking guidance from him from time to time, and he had to confess he liked that. She would definitely need his help in negotiating the glamorous world his work had made him a part of, and he hoped she would see it as the most incredible asset. And if she was ever intimidated or unsure, Seth would be there to help her.

'What an amazing place,' she remarked, glancing round. 'It's so beautiful!'

'I agree. Its reputation surpasses itself. The decor and ambience are superlative, and so is the cuisine. If you've never experienced coming anywhere like this before, it's a very fitting introduction.'

His glance swept over her once again. He privately thought that the lawn-green dress he'd bought her was the perfect foil for her innocent and youthful beauty. His eye for what was both stylish and classy hadn't failed him. Tonight the brunette was positively glowing. And although Seth guessed that a couple of their fellow diners had recognised him, he noted that they were appraising Imogen just as much.

Telling himself that it was inevitable—who *wouldn't* enjoy looking at her?—he smiled up at the attentive blonde waitress who had arrived at their table with the menus and asked, 'Can you give us a little bit longer before you take our order? Then we'll select the wine.'

'But of course, Mr Broden. The sommelier is already waiting to serve you, and if there's anything else you'd like please let me know.'

When they had chosen their dishes, and Seth had selected a suitable wine, he directed his attention back to Imogen. 'I've had the agreement for our marriage drawn up today by my solicitor,' he said, 'and I've had a copy made for you to look over. When you've read it, you can sign the original.'

The smooth skin between her delicately arched brows puckered. 'I told my boss that I might be handing in my notice soon. She was very surprised when I told her why.'

'Because you're getting married or because it's to me?'

'Both. I *had* to tell her who you were—especially as she'll be looking over the agreement with me. But don't worry—she won't tell anyone. In her profession she has to be discreet.'

'It will inevitably come out sooner or later. We'll both have to learn to handle it.'

'Will *your* friends and colleagues be surprised that you're getting married?'

Linking his hands and resting them on the table, he lifted the corners of his mouth with a touch of irony. 'The people who know me call me the Ice Man. It's not meant to be insulting. It's just that it's common knowledge that I'm not swayed by my emotions, either in business or in my private life. I've certainly never professed to being interested in one particular woman, so it will definitely come as a surprise when they find out I've got married!'

Looking hesitant, Imogen asked softly, 'Do any of them know what happened…before you went to the States, I mean?'

Seth handled the flare of disagreeable discomfort that erupted inside him and then ignored it. 'No. There's been no need to tell anyone.'

'Not even any of the women you've dated? Most females I know would want to express their sympathy and offer consolation if you told them.'

'I make it a point not to discuss my past. I prefer to keep my focus on whatever's going on in the present. Besides, my relationships don't tend to be deep and meaningful. They happen purely to fulfil a mutual need.'

He stared into the dark brown depths of her gaze and was aware that he was challenging her to contest the admission. She didn't rise to the bait.

Reminding him of the quintessential, very 'proper' English school prefect, she lifted her chin and said, 'I'm not going to comment on that. But I *would* like to know how you could bear not telling anybody about what happened to Louisa. It was such a significant event in your life.'

He stiffened as his heart momentarily thudded. 'I didn't need to talk to anyone about it. I handled things in my own way and didn't need to look for sympathy. Let's drop the subject, shall we?'

Imogen knew it wasn't the time or the place to persuade Seth to talk some more about his heartache at losing the love of his life, but she wanted to.

Yes, it must be painful beyond imagining, but how

was he going to move on if he didn't lay the ghosts of the past to rest and concentrate on creating a new and more positive chapter in his life? After all, he had grieved for ten long years, and Imogen was going to play a major part in this new phase of his life when they got married. She wanted to help make things good for both of them if she could.

Thankfully, their food arrived at exactly the right moment to prevent the atmosphere from souring, and Seth was diverted as he enthusiastically told her about the exquisite cuisine. He loved the artistry of the creation that went into it, he explained, and Imogen soon intuited that whatever he applied himself to—whether it was selling the most desirable cars in the world or choosing a beautiful dress for his girlfriend—he would do so with the confidence only gifted to the lucky few.

As they sat and enjoyed their food he continued to impress her when he relayed the story of the building's history and why it had become so famous throughout the world. But even as he transfixed her with the breadth of his knowledge she couldn't help but be fascinated by the man himself. She was learning to love the rich bass tone of his voice, the way his incredible sapphire eyes crinkled at the corners when he smiled... the way they drew her in and made her not want to look anywhere else.

By the time they got up to leave Imogen was not just heady from the wine she'd drunk, but mesmerised by the magical time she'd spent with Seth...

She'd fallen asleep on the car journey home.

Seth had done likewise when he'd brought her home from Evergreen that first time, and had ended up spending the night on her couch after he'd surrendered to the emotions that had welled up in him when Imogen had given him the letter. Now she had let her own guard down and done the same.

She was surprised when he asked if he could accompany her into the house. He was acting as though he *enjoyed* spending time with her.

Thinking she should at least make him some coffee, she agreed. Flicking on the lamp just inside the door, she remarked, 'I'm sorry I fell asleep like that... I think I drank a little too much wine.'

A faintly teasing smile touched the edges of his mouth. 'You relaxed enough to enjoy yourself. That's not something you should regret.'

'I had a wonderful time.'

'So did I.'

Closing the space between them, Seth reached for her hand and drew her in against his chest. The throb of her heart turned hot and heavy. In fact it thumped so loudly she was convinced he must detect it.

His gaze was intrigued as he asked huskily, 'Do you still feel like adhering to the idea of no intimacy between us, Imogen?'

Pausing, because his arms had gone around her waist and she was only too aware of how seductive his strong, fit body felt next to hers, she breathed out a sigh. She knew her naturally pleased response to him might easily betray her true feelings about that...

Intoxicated by the wine she'd drunk at dinner, and the dangerous attraction that was building inside her, Imogen strove hard to think clearly. 'I think it's sensible to have some boundaries in place as far as that's concerned. After all, this isn't a real relationship. It's a partnership that's come about purely for convenience. That being the case, we can't afford to make it more personal and spoil it.'

She started to pull away, but Seth surprised her by holding her fast. She felt the warmth of his breath drift across her face, scented his masculine cologne and turned worryingly weak. The provocative blue eyes watching her suggested that he was amused and aroused at the same time.

'What's wrong with us enjoying a little intimacy? We shouldn't deny our natural needs. It might even make the arrangement more compelling if we gave in to them.'

'And it might also complicate things…*big time.*'

Frowning, Seth drawled lazily, 'Just exactly what are you afraid of, Imogen?'

His questions were getting too close for comfort and, wanting to divert him, she retaliated. 'I might ask you the same question. Is it honestly true that you never feel like engaging your emotions? Why is that? Is it because you're afraid you'll get hurt?'

He immediately released her and stepped away. There was a slight flush beneath his cheekbones. 'I put myself wholeheartedly into a relationship that damaged me in more ways than one. Not only was the love of my life killed in a devastating accident, but in the lead-up to that I was belittled and scorned by her father. I vowed never to put myself in such a predicament again. Instead, I focused on becoming successful. I won't ever let anyone degrade me again, nor give my power away by being at the mercy of my feelings.'

CHAPTER SEVEN

'I SEE.' HEARING THE pain and regret in his voice, Imogen honestly felt for him. Having to endure both those things would surely come close to seriously damaging anyone.

But Seth wasn't in the mood for her commiserations. 'Do you?' he flashed irritably. 'I've answered your question. Now why don't you answer mine?'

She could see that she wasn't going to wriggle out of this easily. She could tell that Seth had already somehow intuited exactly what was on her mind. Had he gleaned that she was far more inexperienced than a woman of her age usually was? If he had, he was *right*.

The truth was that she'd kept herself untouched for her wedding night. Since she was very young she'd nursed the romantic notion of giving her virginity to her husband—the man she loved. If she respected herself in that way, then surely the man in her life would, too. She wouldn't end up with a loser, as her poor mum had.

But after what had happened with Greg her once heartfelt wish now seemed like a joke. When they'd been together he'd frequently tried to persuade her to have sex, but she'd always refused. Whilst he'd appreciated that she had certain principles, he'd said that it was wrong of her to deny him what was only natural. He'd been furious and frustrated, but she had somehow convinced herself that he would be more than pleased that she'd kept to her vow on their wedding night.

Her sacrosanct promise had backfired on her. He'd been driven into the arms of another woman, cruelly paying her back for not giving him what he wanted.

It wasn't the first time she'd reflected on these events since being jilted at the altar, and every day the memory seemed heavier. It had devastated her that Greg hadn't seen the innocence she'd offered him as the gift she'd intended it to be.

Glancing back into Seth's crystalline gaze, she brought herself firmly back to the present. Jutting her chin, she declared, 'I'm not afraid.'

He lowered his voice. 'I think you're lying.'

It wasn't an insult. His tone was kind. But as he returned to her, using his long, artistic fingers to comb back her hair, his touch was almost unbearably seductive.

Transfixed, she replied, 'I'm just confused. First you tell me that you want me to be your paid companion. Then you say that I shouldn't feel any pressure about making our relationship intimate, that we should wait and see how things unfold... But now you seem to have changed your mind and you think that we should—we should...'

'Become lovers?'

'Yes.'

'Would that really be so abhorrent?'

Imogen strangely felt like crying. Would this handsome and incredibly successful man of the world even *believe* her if she confessed that she was a virgin? Would he tell her that she was ridiculously naive, saving herself for her wedding night, that such a quaint idea didn't belong in the twenty-first century?

She moved her tongue over her lips to moisten them. 'I'm sure it wouldn't, but it would be crossing a line I told myself I wouldn't cross,' she answered.

'Why? Because you're scared I might be using you? A man in my position doesn't *have* to use women, sweetheart. And I certainly wouldn't try to trap you in that way.' Expelling a sigh, he shook his head thoughtfully. 'Just because we're entering into what is ostensibly a business arrangement doesn't mean we have to suppress our natural instincts. Why don't you think about what I've said and mull it over? I'm not saying we should take things further tonight—all I'm saying is that it would be a fitting way to end a lovely evening if we kissed.'

She couldn't deny that she desperately *wanted* him to kiss her. It seemed to be the case that whenever Seth was within a few feet of her it was all she could think about.

Because she couldn't help herself, she lifted her hand to touch his face delicately. To her intense pleasure she discovered that even the five-o'clock shadow on his cheek had the texture of burnished velvet.

She shouldn't fear his getting closer, she told herself. Even in the short time that she'd known him, Imogen had come to know that Seth was nothing like Greg. For one thing, it seemed to be very important to him to be honest. Maybe, given time, he would even agree to tell her a bit more about the woman he'd loved and lost so cruelly.

'I want you to set the pace, sweetheart, but be aware that you're already testing that decision to the max,' he admitted candidly. 'Do you have *any* idea what your body does for that dress? When I first saw you I thought you were very sweet and young. Now I can see that you're undoubtedly a woman…a very sexy woman…'

In the next moment he was laying his lips against hers and passionately taking her mouth. With a helpless gasp Imogen greedily opened for him, taking his hot silken tongue inside and meeting it with her own. It was the most heavenly kiss she'd ever experienced.

He was moving his hands down her back in the exquisite silk gown. They went straight to her hips and cupped them, drawing her against him. The sensation was so intimate they might have been naked together. The heat he aroused was explosive. It was akin to witnessing the incredible firework display in London on New Year's Eve. Into the dark blazed a melee of kaleidoscope colour that absolutely dazzled her.

As he brought her even closer with an undeniable thrill, she felt the hard ridge behind his fly and knew that she wanted more…*much* more. But somewhere in the middle of the shocking revelation that she wanted to give herself to him body and soul, she felt her eyes welling up with tears. A hot stream slid unchecked down her face and Imogen knew that Seth had tasted them on his lips.

'Hey…' Holding her away, he lightly gripped her shoulders. 'Why are you crying?' He sounded perturbed.

'I suppose I'm feeling a bit emotional. But you don't

believe in that, do you? Giving in to emotion, I mean?'
She didn't disguise her accusatory tone.

'Do you think I'm so hard that I wouldn't care if
you're upset? What's wrong? Will you tell me?'

Imogen knew he must see the tussle going on behind her eyes. Her heartbeat was going crazy. 'I can
tell you... But I'm not sure whether you're going to
like it, or even if you'll believe me.'

'Try me.'

Folding her arms across the exquisite silk of her
dress, she determinedly met his gaze. 'My fiancé stood
me up at the altar because I wouldn't have sex with him
before we married. He paid me back by cheating on me
with another woman and chose to leave me standing
there to make me look like a fool. Then he refused to
return my share of the deposit on our house because
he said I didn't deserve it. It was *my* fault that everything had gone so wrong.' She shuddered. 'What I'm
trying to tell you is that I'm a virgin, Seth.'

Now she *really* had his attention. 'You were saving
yourself for your husband? Is that what you mean?'

Forlornly, Imogen nodded. 'Yes...'

'Was it a matter of principle that you refused him
sex?'

Squirming, she sensed her cheeks flush heatedly.
'I had good reason. When my mum got pregnant with
me my father immediately told her that he was married. Then he admitted that he'd seen their relationship
as "a little bit of fun" on the side. After that he walked
away as if he didn't have a care in the world. Because
of what happened to her I vowed I would never be so
easily duped by a man, and that I wouldn't sleep with
anyone until I was sure. I wanted someone I could

trust…someone who would be glad to honour his responsibilities to both me and to our children if we were to have them.

'When I fell for Greg I held on to those beliefs. I honestly thought that our union would mean so much more if we waited until we were married. At first he liked the idea. But then…then he started to show his frustration.'

'Like I said before, you're well rid of the man. You deserve better—that's why it didn't work out. Not because you did something wrong.'

'I totally understand if you want to call off our deal…'

Seth's brow creased in disbelief. 'Why on earth would I want to do *that*?'

'Because I'm not experienced in the way most women my age are. If we get together, like you suggested, I would probably disappoint you. And, whilst I know you want me mainly as a companion, I honestly don't know how I'd cope if we slept together and then you sought pleasure with other women because I didn't please you.'

With an audible sigh Seth took her into his arms, and the look he gave her was intense. 'It's not just about pleasing *me*, Imogen. If and when we make love it will be a two-way street. Your pleasure is equally important—even more so in light of what you've just told me.'

His words filled her with elation. Maybe their proposed partnership *would* turn out to be a good thing. If she could learn to trust that he was sincere she might be able lower the protective barriers she'd erected round her heart and enjoy life once again…

'I think that we need to get this marriage arranged sooner rather than later,' he announced firmly. 'Leave it to me. I have contacts who can help us. In the meantime, I want you to organise to take next week off. I'm going to take you away somewhere for a little holiday, so that we can really start to get to know one another without distraction.'

His blue eyes crinkled at the corners, as they were apt to do whenever he smiled that knee-buckling smile of his, and Imogen's limbs turned as weak as marshmallow.

'Just one more kiss,' he said. 'Then I have to go and you can get to bed.'

As soon as the hot, sultry kiss began she knew she didn't want it to end. As his hands moved down over her body Seth made her feel things that she'd never felt before—even at the height of her ultimately disastrous romance with Greg. His touch stoked a fire in her that flamed hotter as each moment passed.

He cupped her breast through the flimsy material of her dress and teased the nipple into burgeoning life, then he nipped at her mouth with his teeth, making her gasp. But suddenly, with a groan, he fastened his hands round her slim upper arms and called a halt to the proceedings. Both of them were breathing hard.

'As much as I'd like to stay, I think we need to rein things in,' he told her huskily. 'When we do finally make love I want it to be in surroundings more conducive to relaxation—somewhere beautiful. I'll ring you in a couple of days and let you know about the arrangements for our trip. Now I'll go and get your passport and birth certificate from the car, and I'll also get the copy of the marriage agreement that I had drawn up.'

He left her for a while to do just that, and Imogen hugged her arms over her chest in a bid to try to stay calm. Even when Seth left her for the shortest time she felt as if something vital was missing.

He quickly returned and left the documents on the coffee table. With a slow smile he clasped her to him and kissed her cheek. 'Remember that you're going to need to take the whole week off.'

'I know. I won't forget.'

'Good.'

True to his word, but with clear reluctance, Seth left her then, and Imogen sank down onto the couch, hardly knowing what to make of her growing feelings for this man. Her lips were aching and contused after their hungry caresses, and her body was frustrated beyond belief that she hadn't been able to attain fulfilment.

She couldn't believe how much she craved his touch. He had made her feel more alive than she'd felt in *years*, and her blood was infused with dizzying heat when she thought about their getting to know one another more intimately in the week that would follow...

Hardly a moment went by over the next couple of days when Seth *didn't* find himself thinking about Imogen.

His surprise that she could have such a profound effect on him was genuine. Usually he made a point of never letting a woman get into his blood to such a disturbing degree, but just one glance from her lovely brown eyes had the power to make him forget that vow and long to know her intimately. Especially since he had tasted the sweetly drugging nectar of her lips and experienced the delightful curves of her body beneath his hands...

Learning that she was a virgin had explained why she had that beguiling air of untouched innocence about her, and his heart had raced when she'd told him that she wanted to stay pure for her wedding night. This so-called 'convenient' arrangement he was contemplating now had the potential to turn into something far more serious if he didn't take things more slowly.

That was why he didn't trust emotions. They were apt to make people fall into making rash decisions that could adversely impact on them for the rest of their lives. Whilst he couldn't ever regret falling for Louisa all those years ago, the way her father had made him feel so small and unworthy was a stain on his soul that wouldn't easily be removed.

But Imogen was a real rarity in this day and age, that was for sure. And because her innocence wasn't something he took at all lightly, it would be up to him to make her experience of making love for the very first time satisfyingly memorable and one she wouldn't regret...

It was one night in the middle of the week before Seth called her to confirm the details of their vacation. The demands of his day had been relentless. As well as driving into London for another meeting at the Lamborghini dealership, and being introduced to two important new clients there, he had been firming up the details of their marriage with the agency he'd hired to organise the wedding and finalising the arrangements for their trip away, It felt as if he had hardly stopped to draw breath.

It came as no surprise when Imogen confessed that she'd gone to bed. She hadn't expected him to be ringing so late.

Glancing at his watch, he realised she was right. It was *very* late. 'Sorry about that.' He grimaced. 'I feel as if I've been on rails today. I haven't stopped.'

'That can't be good for you...'

He heard her stifle a yawn.

'A body needs rest as well as activity. Did you get something proper to eat?'

Seth didn't answer straight away, because the sleepy cadence of her voice was seriously making him tingle. It didn't help that he couldn't help wondering what kind of nightwear she wore to bed—if she wore any at all. There wasn't one other woman in his sphere who dispensed care and concern as she did. It was a revelation that such a quality could be so alluring.

Gravel voiced, he replied, 'Yes, I did. I sent out for a sandwich during my meeting.'

'You only had a *sandwich*?'

'That's all I needed.'

'Surely just a sandwich won't give you the energy you need when you're working?'

'It was good enough.'

'You should have gone out and had a proper lunch... that's all I'm saying.'

'Don't be so concerned. Do I look as if I'm in need of feeding?'

'I don't deny that you certainly *look* pretty fit and strong...'

Grinning with satisfaction, and not a little male pride, Seth commented, 'So you've observed that about me, have you?'

At the other end of the phone it went ominously quiet.

'Imogen...are you still there?'

She sighed, and it was as though the warmth of her breath drifted through the telephone and touched his cheek.

'Yes. I'm still here. Was there a particular reason for your call?'

'I wanted to tell you about the arrangements for our trip.'

'You've decided where we're going, then?'

'Yes, I have.'

'So where's it going to be?'

'I'm not going to tell you the destination because I want it to be a surprise. All you need to know is that we'll be leaving early on Saturday. I'll come to the house around eight to collect you. Bring an assortment of clothing in case we have to contend with bad weather at some point.'

'Okay...'

'You still trust me not to do wrong by you, don't you?'

Seth found it hard to keep the doubt from his voice. There was always the potential that Imogen might change her mind about their deal. He hadn't forgotten that she'd warned him about that. He wished he'd gone to the house to see her face-to-face rather than rely on the phone.

'I do. I'll make sure I'm ready on time.'

'Good.' Low voiced, he confessed, 'I've missed not seeing you these past couple of days, you know...'

'You mean you're not regretting asking me to marry you?'

'Absolutely not!'

'Well, then...'

Hearing the distinct smile in her voice, he was satisfied that she wasn't going to back out after all.

'I'll see you on Saturday.'

'Goodnight, Imogen. I'd better let you get some sleep.'

'Goodnight, Seth. Make sure you get some rest, too. Even Superman must have had to have some downtime now and again, to recharge his batteries.'

Chuckling, he rang off, knowing that it would be *her* face that he took with him into sleep that night and no one else's.

He was surprised at how reassured he felt about that…

Saturday arrived, and Imogen had been on tenterhooks from the early hours, knowing that today she was going away with Seth. She'd been up and dressed at the crack of dawn, and now busied herself making some last-minute checks on her packing as she nervously waited for his arrival.

She attested to feeling as Fanny Robin must have done in *Far From the Madding Crowd*, when her sweetheart Troy hadn't appeared because she'd been waiting for him at the wrong church… She knew what it was like to be stood up on what was supposed to be the happiest day of a woman's life, and—dear God—she didn't want to experience such a devastating scenario again.

Seth *would* show up so they could go away together, *wouldn't* he?

She was checking her appearance in the sitting room mirror, trying to maintain her optimism and miserably failing, when a loud thump on the front door—the bell still hadn't been repaired—signalled that her visitor had arrived. Even as she stared into the mirror she saw the cherry-bright colour that seeped into her cheeks.

Turning away, she whispered, 'Thank God he kept his word...' and hurried out into the hallway to let him in.

He looked wonderful. Scratch that. It wasn't just the fact that he *looked* amazing that overwhelmed her, but the sheer charisma he exuded that stole her breath. Wearing another immaculate tailored grey suit, he wasn't a man anyone could ignore. With his sculpted features and chiselled jaw he was as handsome as ever, and even at such an early hour his dazzling blue eyes shone with an almost preternatural brightness that rendered Imogen as weak as a kitten as she stared back at him.

His gaze was unwaveringly direct... 'Hi.'

'Hi,' she greeted him back. 'You made it on time, then?'

'Did you doubt that I would?'

'Why don't you come in? It looks cold out there.'

Not answering his question, she let him inside the hallway and when she'd shut the door stole one or two precious moments to try to steady her nerves.

This was no small undertaking she was embarking on, and Seth needed to know that. More important, she didn't want him to believe that her agreement to marry him meant that he would have everything his own way. Whatever happened, she was determined to make her own needs important, too...

CHAPTER EIGHT

To IMOGEN'S SURPRISE, Seth drove them to a heliport just a few miles away. Whilst she'd guessed they would be flying somewhere, she'd assumed they'd be going to an airport to board a plane. But confronted with the reality of this alternative form of transport, she felt her insides catapulting with excitement. She'd never experienced travelling in a helicopter before and viewed it as an unexpected bonus.

But as soon as the silver-haired pilot had lifted off she clutched her hands in her lap and fell silent. She wasn't nervous about the flying. Even the noise of the whirring blades and the sudden jolting ascent didn't bother her. It was just that the scenario she found herself in was so far away from her usual day-to-day experience that she had to pinch herself to believe that it was really happening.

The most surprising thing of all was that she was accompanying a wealthy and supremely confident businessman who'd barely been in her life five minutes, and that somehow she'd agreed to become his wife in a marriage of convenience…

'It's a good feeling to be on our way,' Seth commented, turning in his seat to glance at her. 'With no obstacles to delay us. It's been my experience in my career that something usually comes up at the last minute.'

Imogen screwed up her face. 'Don't say that. It might be unlucky.'

'Are you telling me that you're superstitious?'

'I've been known to avoid the number thirteen and walking under ladders—that kind of thing.'

Amused, he shook his head. 'Well, nothing's going to spoil our trip. Trust me.'

Inexplicably, and going against all her usual instincts, she *did*. 'Are you going to tell me where we're going now?'

He smiled. 'I suppose I ought to. You've done well not to press me for answers so far. Women's curiosity usually gets the better of them, I've found. We're going to Scotland. I hope you took my advice and packed some clothes for inclement weather?'

'I did. I even packed a pair of sturdy boots in case we went walking. You can probably tell I was in the Girl Guides. My motto is Be Prepared.'

A painful reminder that she hadn't been remotely prepared for being jilted at the altar made her insides tighten disagreeably. Quickly corralling the emotion, she quelled it, knowing that it would only spoil things.

'But I never guessed we might be going to Scotland. What made you choose that for our destination?'

'Wait until we get there and I'll explain. In the meantime why don't you just kick back and enjoy the ride? You're going to see some amazing scenery en route.'

'Okay, I will.'

The views over England were stunning enough, but as they left them behind and travelled further north her gaze encountered a proliferation of mountains, woodlands and reed beds in abundance. It was magical to see the narrow rivers that wove in and out through the differing habitats, the glint of diamond-bright sunlight on the shimmering water clearly marking them out.

The further afield they travelled, the more the colours of the land changed, too. She'd never realised before how many different shades of green there were. And every now and then the verdant shades were interspersed by acres of stunning purple heather.

In what seemed like hardly any time at all the pilot told them to prepare for landing. Keeping her sights fixed on the scenery as the helicopter descended, Imogen saw a flat, rugged landscape, with the most stunning backdrop of mountains rising up behind it, and a rush of pleasure soared through her.

The sensation was deliciously heightened when Seth curled his hand round hers. 'Put your coat on,' he advised. 'It's bound to be cold.'

The pilot turned to address them. 'Here we are, Mr Broden. If you'd like to disembark, I'll bring out your luggage.'

'Thank you, Patrick.'

As soon as they were outside the helicopter a raw and icy wind made Imogen's breath catch. Seth had been right about the drop in temperature. It was absolutely freezing. Arranging the hood of her parka with its faux fur edging more closely round her face, she felt her teeth chatter helplessly.

In contrast, *he* didn't look remotely put out by the icy temperature. He had merely thrown a Burberry mackintosh over his immaculate suit, and he had the look of a suave male model about to be photographed to promote a very exclusive brand of cologne.

'I hope that you and your young lady have a wonderful time here.' Patrick warmly shook Seth's hand and then Imogen's.

Had she imagined it, or had there been a distinct twinkle in the man's eyes when he'd glanced back at her? Did he perhaps know something that she didn't?

There was no time to ponder, because suddenly a uniformed young couple were upon them—the man expertly arranging their luggage on a wheeled trolley as his pretty companion warmly welcomed them, announcing that her name was Nina. Then she asked them to follow her to the hotel.

Suddenly Imogen found that she had a myriad of questions to ask Seth. She still couldn't fathom why he'd chosen Scotland for their first trip together. But he was looking straight ahead, as if he had more than enough on his mind to occupy him and wasn't up for answering questions.

Then, as if intuiting that she was a little unsettled, he lightly touched his hand to her back as they walked towards the gracious nineteenth-century building that was their hotel.

'If you'd like to come with me into Reception, the staff will check you in, and then I'll show you and Miss Hayes to your suite, Mr Broden. In the meantime a porter will take your luggage up to the rooms.'

'Thank you.'

'You're most welcome,' Nina replied.

The young female concierge blushed as she met Seth's arresting blue eyes, and Imogen completely understood why the woman suddenly appeared flustered.

As they travelled in the elevator up to their suite she deliberately avoided Seth's examining gaze. She was suddenly struck dumb by what she was about to do.

Even though the kisses they'd shared were the most arousing she'd ever experienced, and had reassured her that she would have no trouble being turned on by him in bed, she was understandably apprehensive because she'd never spent the night with a man before. To some degree it helped that her handsome companion was aware of that, but still it didn't dispel the nervousness she felt about taking things much further.

When the charming concierge had been duly thanked and tipped, she smilingly departed. Turning together, Imogen and Seth surveyed their luxurious surroundings.

'So this is how the other half live?' she quipped.

A smile touched her companion's lips but he didn't comment.

The suite door opened on to a gracious sitting room decorated in tastefully muted tones of cream and mint green. It was furnished with two generous-size spruce-coloured velvet sofas and a pair of cream armchairs arranged round an art deco coffee table.

Murmuring that it was all lovely, Imogen saw that Seth was already moving into the main bedroom to examine it. She followed him more slowly. When she arrived, for a disconcerting moment she couldn't take her eyes off the large four-poster bed that dominated the room, draped with sumptuous cranberry and lilac silks and an array of vintage-style cushions. It came to her that it wouldn't look out of place in a sheikh's harem.

'You can sleep in here tonight. I'll take the spare bed next door,' her companion announced casually.

Glancing up at him, Imogen frowned. 'It doesn't seem right that I should have it all to myself.'

'It's only for tonight. You won't be on your own tomorrow.'

'No?'

Holding her gaze, Seth went still. 'We're getting married... Tomorrow night we'll be husband and wife.'

At the realisation that she would be losing her virginity sooner than she'd thought, Imogen couldn't seem to find the wherewithal to reply. Once again a powerful sense of unreality washed over her.

'You mean that we're going to be married *here*?' she asked, the words catching in her throat.

Lifting a gently mocking eyebrow, Seth nodded. 'This *is* Gretna Green. It's what the place is famous for.'

'I didn't realise... I think—I think I need to sit down.' Dazed, she moved across the room to an armchair.

Her companion followed her. 'It's all been arranged, Imogen. This is the surprise I promised you. I've even arranged the dress that you'll be wearing. You said you like vintage, so that's the style I've chosen for you. The designer will be joining us later, so that you can try it on and she can make any last-minute adjustments.'

'What about the witnesses we'll need for the ceremony? Have you organised them, too?'

'Yes. The hotel's manager and our female concierge Nina have agreed to help us out. Do you mind that you won't have any personal friends or family present? Only I had to organise things quickly...'

Breathing out a sigh, Imogen undid her parka and took it off. Then she dropped down into the wing-backed armchair behind her. Exceptionally comfortable, it made the one she had at home seem particularly old and worn. 'I don't mind. It's probably best that they won't be here.'

'Why's that?'

'I suppose I don't want to face their judgement or disapproval—particularly my mum's. Like I said, she's had so much disappointment in her life. And I seem to have acquired a reputation for not exactly making the best decisions. She wouldn't fail to remind me of that.'

'Then, I'm glad your people won't be joining us.'

Frowning, Seth followed her example and undid his jacket. He deposited the expensive-looking garment onto the lavishly covered bed.

'What about you? Don't *you* have any friends or family who might be interested in the fact that you're getting married?'

His jaw visibly clenched. 'No. I don't.'

Imogen couldn't help but challenge his answer. 'Would they be interested if this marriage was for real?'

Flinching as though struck, he rubbed a hand round his jaw. 'By that I take it you mean if we were in love?'

There was no mockery in his tone, but she couldn't fail to hear the note of derision at the concept that was there, and her throat cramped painfully. It hurt to remember that their proposed union was certainly no love match but merely one of convenience. She should never forget that.

'Anyway...' Forcing a smile to save him from stating the obvious and convince him that she wasn't disturbed that their marriage wouldn't be for real, she asked, 'What time will the designer bring my dress?'

'She'll be here soon—in about an hour.'

'One more question. Where exactly will the ceremony take place?'

A flash of pleasure lit the compelling blue irises as he told her, 'It's going to be conducted in the ancient Chief's Room situated in a five-hundred-year-old Peel Tower. I'm told that the stone walls are decorated with portraits of previous lairds, like Robert the Bruce. There's also a valuable and historic Persian rug covering the flagstone floor.'

It sounded beautiful and romantic—just the kind of atmospheric venue where a woman in love might enjoy being married, Imogen thought with a pang. 'I get the feeling that you love history?'

'I do. I've loved it since I was a boy. In another life I might have studied it. Anyway, I'd like to take a shower now—how about you?'

'I—I...' Her head throbbed in alarm.

'Not together.' Good humour returned, Seth grinned. 'At least not yet. Do you want to take one first?'

Garnering all her courage, she squarely met his gaze. 'You can go first. I think I'll start my unpacking.'

His contemplative glance lingered a little too long for it to be remotely comfortable. Was he perhaps regretting his decision to ask her to marry him?

As if suddenly realising that he was staring, he declared, 'Okay. I won't be long.' Turning, he disappeared through one of the maple-wood doors to the luxurious bathroom and shower the concierge had shown them.

When he had gone Imogen fully intended to go and unlock her suitcase, but she found herself slumping back in the chair instead. Staring at nothing in particular, she reminded herself that she was getting married *tomorrow*—to a man who had wealth, charisma and generosity in spades, but whose heart was frozen in time because he'd pledged it when he was young to a girl who had tragically lost her life…

Leaning his hands against the white marble surround that housed the generously sized bathroom sinks, Seth didn't immediately undress for his shower.

On this, the day before his marriage, memories of Louisa were inevitable. For a while he became lost in them. Old feelings stirred. He recalled how he had loved everything about her—from her long red hair and haunting green eyes to her courage in standing up to her peers when they'd mocked where he came from because it was a notoriously 'lowly' part of town.

He had been quite capable of putting them straight himself, but he had known such confrontations would inevitably spark his temper and likely end in somebody getting a bloody nose, so by and large he'd avoided the possibility.

Even when his mood had been morose Louisa had always found a way to make him smile. Most of all she had made him feel loved and accepted, and had helped ease the ache in his soul brought about by his father's cruel and drunken behaviour.

He had regularly sworn at Seth, telling him that he was a mistake and his mother was a whore. How he would have loved to have had the physique he had now, to square up to him and throw him out of the house. He had attempted to do just that on a couple of occasions but had ended up in A&E for his troubles, with his distraught mother begging him never to try it again. As fate would have it, shortly after Louisa had died his father had died suddenly from a heart attack.

Years later, when Seth had started to make substantial amounts of money from his endeavours in America, he had sent his mother the money to buy a house. These days she lived quietly, deep in the Welsh countryside. And she professed to love the peace and quiet over being with another man. Who could blame her?

His thoughts returned to Louisa. Seth knew he would have married her if she'd lived. Staring at his reflection in the mirror, and noting one or two strands of grey in his hair, he thought about how frighteningly fast the years had passed. Then, as if waking from a dream, his thoughts turned to this 'marriage of convenience' that lay ahead of him.

His ensuing sigh was heavy. What he'd believed was the obvious solution to ending the soulless existence he'd long endured without a female partner to 'humanise' him was starting to appear more complicated than he'd envisaged. For a start, he found himself more attracted to Imogen than was entirely sensible. And—dare he say it?—he'd discovered that he cared what she thought about their arrangement a little too much.

Yes, he brought some attractive assets to the table—like his wealth and position—but would that be enough to satisfy her? He was quickly beginning to realise that she shared some of the same appealing qualities Louisa had had, in that she didn't appear to be driven by the material things in life.

The last thing he wanted to do was make her feel pressured into marrying him. The woman had already been hurt beyond measure by her ex-fiancé. Yet when those soulful dark eyes of hers glimmered with delight at some inconsequential thing he said or did, and she smiled up at him as if he'd hung the moon, Seth forgot everything but his desire to hold her tight and make love to her.

Was that how she had looked at her faithless ex? he wondered.

More irritated than he cared to own at the thought, he pushed his fingers irritably through his hair. Deciding it was best if he kept his mind on the rules he and Imogen had agreed about their upcoming partnership—that it was to be a union forged out of mutual convenience and *not* one where they engaged their emotions—Seth turned on the shower and hastily stripped off his clothes...

He'd come down to the lobby to meet the designer he had hired to deliver and fit Imogen's dress for the wedding. Celia Bamford was an attractive middle-aged woman, with flashes of hot pink amongst the silver of her stylish short hair, and she had an impressive clientele that included some of the younger royals.

Whilst Seth would have preferred to have had a dress made exclusively for his wife-to-be, time and circumstance had prevented it. Consequently he had had to choose from a select array of garments that the designer had already created to show to potential customers. Fortunately he'd found one that in his opinion perfectly complemented Imogen's delicate frame and features.

He had done well to get Celia Bamford's services at such short notice, even though he was well aware that his name and reputation had clinched the deal.

After the introductions were over Seth was eager for his guest to meet Imogen and, instructing a porter to bring the ornately boxed dress to the suite, he accompanied Celia up to their floor in the elevator.

Wearing skinny jeans that lovingly clung in all the right places and an emerald-green T-shirt that highlighted the alluring curve of her breasts, Imogen answered the door when Seth knocked. Seeing that she'd washed and dried her hair in his absence, he noted how the chestnut-brown ringlets cascaded delightfully down over her shoulders like a magical waterfall from a fairy tale.

A jolt of disturbing awareness ricocheted through his insides as he registered how young she looked. Young, innocent and perhaps too easily taken advantage of...

Quelling the sense of guilt that gripped him, he stood back to introduce the designer. 'Imogen, this is Celia Bamford, who has designed the dress you'll be wearing at the ceremony. Celia—this is my fiancée, Imogen.'

Right on cue the porter knocked at the door, and Seth took delivery of the box that contained the all-important wedding finery.

When the man had left, the designer exclaimed, 'My dear...you're even lovelier than I'd hoped you'd be!'

Although her exclamation was a tad theatrical, she clasped Imogen to her in what appeared to be genuine delight. When she released her Seth saw the familiar rosy hue that invaded the younger woman's cheeks and felt immediately protective.

Catching her hand, he pulled her to him and brushed her cheek with his lips. The gesture reminded him of how infinitely soft her skin was. Already he was having withdrawal symptoms because it had been too long since he'd touched her, he realised.

'She's telling the truth. You *are* lovely. I only hope the dress I've chosen will do justice to your beauty.'

He heard the soft intake of breath she took just before her cheeks dimpled. 'People always say nice things about the bride, don't they? They should spare a compliment or two for the groom.'

Celia nodded in agreement. 'You're *so* right, Imogen. There won't be one female heart that doesn't leap with pleasure when they see your handsome husband-to-be dressed in his tux at the wedding.'

'There won't be many guests at the ceremony,' Seth commented soberly. 'It was a last-minute arrangement.'

'Oh...'

Beneath her perfectly applied make-up, it was easy to detect the immediate conclusion the designer had come to. She couldn't know how ironic that was when in fact he hadn't even bedded Imogen yet... Still, he couldn't deny that the idea of her carrying his baby was suddenly inexplicably appealing. Why *was* that? he mused.

'What a shame that all your friends and family won't see you both in your finery,' Celia declared. 'Still, I'm sure it won't be long before you can celebrate with them when you get home.'

'My main concern is that my fiancée gets what she needs. Right now I'm not thinking about anyone else.'

The designer recovered from the blunt statement Seth had made commendably quickly.

Patting down her colourful bob, she remarked, 'I understand. Of course I do. It's only right that your focus should be on each other at such an important time. So, if you'd be kind enough to leave Imogen and me for a while, Mr Broden, she can try on the dress and I can start to make any adjustments I need to make.'

'Good.'

Catching Imogen's eye with a conspiratorial wink as he started to move towards the door, Seth fervently hoped the dress he'd chosen for her would please her and help her feel especially beautiful on the day they got married...

CHAPTER NINE

IMOGEN HARDLY RECOGNISED the vision that confronted her in the tall boudoir mirror. Was that really her? The wedding dress that Seth had chosen for her was created out of the most delicate ivory French lace, its folds and bodice tastefully decorated with lilac crystals and fragile seed pearls. And, best of all, its design was faithfully vintage.

It was the most feminine and beautiful gown she'd ever seen. The sublime material flowed down her legs to her ankles as effortlessly as a river flowed back to its source and, wearing it, she felt like Titania, queen of the fairies, from *A Midsummer's Night Dream*.

'Your fiancé has an enviable eye for what enhances your beauty, Imogen. Only a man who pays attention to the smallest of details could have selected such a dress for his woman. You look utterly exquisite. It complements your figure perfectly.'

Although she no doubt told every bride-to-be that she looked wonderful, Celia Bamford sounded as if she meant every word. It was all a little overwhelming—especially when she referred to Imogen as Seth's 'woman'. It gave her a funny feeling inside. For once in her life she felt as if she *mattered*, as if her feelings were important.

'Thank you. And I have to agree—Seth has very good taste.'

'You're a very lucky woman. But then, *he* is a very fortunate man.'

Smiling, the designer dropped down to her haunches to arrange the gown's material so that it fell exactly the way she wanted it to. She rose again to fuss over the lace bodice, ensuring that the fitting met her exacting standards. It did. Imogen couldn't imagine it being any more perfect.

'Turn and turn again, so I can make sure it's shown to advantage from every angle,' the older woman instructed.

After Imogen had obliged, she asked her to walk away from her and then back again, critically observing every detail of the dress, as though to find even the smallest flaw would herald catastrophe for her reputation and career...

'Now I'm going to arrange the headdress for you. Will you be wearing your hair down tomorrow?'

Imogen nodded. 'I'd prefer to wear it loose. It won't interfere with the design?'

'On the contrary, my dear, in this case the natural look is most definitely the best.'

She breathed a sigh of relief. Celia's reaction reassured her that if *she* thought it the right choice, then it was likely her husband-to-be would, too...

After finishing the outstanding dinner that had been cooked exclusively for them by one of the country's top chefs, and having declined inducements to have coffee and brandy, Seth and Imogen exited the discreet art deco–style dining room. The room was allocated to guests who particularly wanted their privacy, and in accordance with Seth's request they had dined alone.

He had tried to make conversation with Imogen throughout the evening, but she seemed particularly withdrawn tonight. It came to him that she was brooding about something. Alarm bells started to ring. He wouldn't rest until he found out the reason.

Hadn't she liked the dress? Perhaps he had trusted Celia Bamford too readily to help him decide what would suit her?

They were both silent as they travelled back up to the suite. The day had been full of new experiences for her, and Seth silently acknowledged that it must have taken its toll. It was quite likely that she was feeling a little overwhelmed. Once or twice at dinner he'd caught her stifling a yawn. No doubt her emotions were running high about what lay ahead tomorrow.

It wouldn't surprise him if her fears about the wedding possibly *not* going ahead were getting the better of her. After all, it was only a year ago that she'd suffered the ultimate humiliation by her louse of a fiancé. His fists immediately clenched at the thought. He would have to reassure her that it wasn't going to happen a second time, that he had no doubts whatsoever that he was doing the right thing in marrying her.

But even as he had the thought Seth uncomfortably shelved the knowledge that his intention to marry *hadn't* been prompted solely by his desire to have meaningful companionship in his life. It had also been prompted by his friend Ash's suggestion that he get himself a trophy wife. If he wanted the chance to be accepted by the elite coterie of classic-car owners and collectors in his father's kingdom, and add to his list of impressive clientele worldwide, a wife was a *must*.

On entering their suite, Seth saw that the chambermaid had turned on the contemporary wall fire in the sitting room. Behind the toughened glass it had a realistic open-fire effect that made for a very pleasing ambience. The brocade plum curtains had also been closed, and the lighting in the lamps had been adjusted so that it was intimately subtle.

The atmosphere couldn't help but turn Seth's mind to seduction... He was only too aware that his body heat—already on simmer whenever he was anywhere *near* the brown-eyed beauty who was his fiancée—had just gone up several notches.

'Why don't you kick off your shoes and sit down? You need to relax... It's been a long day,' he remarked, loosening his tie and moving towards her.

Tonight, despite the fact that she must be a little overwrought emotionally, Imogen was more beautiful than ever. Wearing black palazzo pants and a white silk tunic that skimmed her svelte hips, with her dark hair curling softly against her shoulders, she was an effortlessly elegant ingénue who had no idea of the profound effect she could have on a man.

Dropping down onto the retro club sofa behind her, she toed off her ebony flats and gave him a disarming smile. 'I agree. It has. I never would have guessed that indulging in pursuits purely for pleasure could make me this tired.'

'Presumably that's because you aren't used to flexing that particular muscle? Tell me—is that the only reason you're tired, Imogen, or is there something else on your mind?'

Her expression veiled, she rose slowly to her feet. A jolt of surprise ricocheted through Seth's insides when she moved to stand right in front of him. The scent of her warm, light perfume was like the petals of exquisite frangipani and indelibly intoxicating.

All of a sudden the air between them was alive with electricity. He had only to stretch out his hand to touch her and he would be able to ease the need that was growing stronger in him by the second. He was beginning to learn that this woman was pure carnal temptation. His blood wasn't merely flowing through his veins…it was *pounding.*

But although her hard-to-resist allure was seriously testing him, he was concerned about what she might be going to say. Was she going to tell him that she'd changed her mind about marrying him? When he realised it was a possibility he sensed his heart racing in protest.

'What is it?'

'It's nothing… I just— I just…'

As she brushed aside her hair where it glanced against her cheek, Imogen's gaze was surprisingly steady. Seth couldn't attest to the fact that he even breathed right then. The look in her eyes had stopped all thought in its tracks. What he saw in those silken burnished depths was a seductive mix of desire, need and longing… All the things he'd secretly yearned for her to feel for him and more…

'What are you trying to do to me?' he husked.

'Don't worry…I just want you to kiss me…'

Whether the gesture was meant or purely unconscious, she moistened her heavenly lips with her tongue.

'Is that allowed on the night before we get married, Seth?'

'We can do whatever we damn well please.'

Hungrily urging her slim body towards his, he held
her head fast and eagerly brought his lips down to hers.
The contact was akin to that magical moment when a
flame was ignited from dry tinder and took hold. The
more he kissed her, the more he wanted to explore the
satin textures of her mouth.

Seth fed the flames of his desire and the sparks spat
and hissed, scorching his skin and burning him. He
had never known such need. Yes, he had known hunger for sexual fulfilment—of course he had—but not
as powerful and fierce as this.

Lifting the filmy material of her blouse aside, he
cupped one full breast and bent down to taste it. When
he'd tugged her white lace bra lower to expose her nipple, his mouth hungrily latched on to it and suckled.
She was salty and sweet, the nipple that swelled beneath his fingers musky and sexy.

The shuddering sigh of pleasure she released left
him in no doubt that she wanted him, and the knowledge made him clutch her even closer. Claiming her
mouth once again, he drove his hips against her belly.
He was hot, hard and aching. He could take her now,
in a heartbeat, he was so turned on.

But just as he was about to direct her towards the
couch so they could be more intimate, Imogen put her
hands on his chest and pressed firmly to halt him.
First she had indicated that she wanted him, but now
it seemed she was cooling things down.

Seth's head throbbed in confusion. 'What's wrong? Isn't this what you wanted…? To be closer?'

She swallowed hard, her gaze nervous. 'Presumably you're talking about being sexually closer but not close in any other way?'

He scowled. 'If you're talking about engaging feelings, I've told you that I prefer not to involve my emotions. Risking that kind of attachment has too many painful connotations for me.'

'Why? Is it because you fear more loss?'

Suddenly Imogen felt much older than her years. The shocking effect of losing the woman he'd adored when he was young had instilled a deep fear into Seth's heart, she guessed… So much so that he didn't want to risk getting close to another woman emotionally in case he somehow lost her, too.

Breathing out a sigh, he studied her thoughtfully for a few moments. 'We all have to take steps to protect ourselves sometimes. But that doesn't mean I won't respect you or take care of your needs, Imogen. I'll do everything I can to ensure that you have a good life… the life you deserve.'

'Let's be frank. Do you still wish it was Louisa that you were marrying, Seth? In that note I found in the book you said that you would never love anyone but her.'

He flinched. She might as well have thrown a bucket of ice water over him. He'd hardly expected her to challenge him about his feelings for Louisa at this stage of the game. In fact having made his intentions clear, he hadn't expected her to ask him about it at all.

Quickly orientating himself, he ground out, 'What's love got to do with it? We've made an agreement that is eminently practical for both of us. Now you seem to be suggesting that you want something more.'

She pursed her lips, and the colour seemed to drain from her face. 'I was simply asking a question. I won't ask you for anything that you don't want to give me, Seth. I just want to be sure of where I stand.'

'Let me turn the tables. Answer me this. Do you wish that your ex had turned up at the church that day? Is it still *him* that you want, Imogen?'

She was appalled that he would think such a thing even for a second. 'I would *never* want to be with him! If he got down on his knees and begged me to take him back my answer would still be no. We were finished long before that ridiculous charade at the church, only I didn't allow myself to admit it. I kept fooling myself that I was in love, but looking back, I realise it was just a fantasy. I'm telling you the truth.'

'And I'm telling *you* the truth. Louisa *died.* Saying I wish it was her I was marrying is utterly futile. I've made the right decision in asking you to be my wife, Imogen... There's no dispute about that. So why don't we both agree to put our pasts aside and move on?'

He hadn't answered her question about never loving anyone else. If she wanted this marriage of convenience to have any hope of working she knew she should probably let things lie. But the idea was even harder after the heated connection they'd just shared.

'*Why* have you made the right decision in deciding to marry me, Seth? Is it because you think I'm docile enough to go along with the marriage and not give you a hard time about the fact that you won't ever engage your feelings?'

He looked genuinely stunned. Imogen could hardly

believe she'd said the words out loud. Her heart was pounding fit to burst.

Shaking his head, Seth ground out, 'I've never thought you docile. As for my feelings…I told you once before that I believe things will unfold, given time, and I honestly believe we'll enjoy a good marriage.'

'Even though it'll be just a marriage of convenience and not one where you feel anything meaningful? What if I decide I don't want to settle for such a cold-sounding deal after all?'

Now he looked shocked. Then he looked angry, and she flinched as his hands fastened tightly round her slim upper arms.

'What are you saying? Our chemistry is combustible. There's nothing "cold" about this deal whatsoever. There are times when we can hardly keep our hands off each other—and don't you dare deny it!'

Imogen *didn't*. When Seth kissed her and touched her the feelings he stirred inside her went way beyond anything she could have dreamed or imagined. He made her feel exhilarated and alive…as if she'd been walking through the world half asleep until she'd met him.

It thrilled her to know that he ached for her. Yet it still hurt more than she could say to know that he would never love her as she wanted him to… *As she loved him*.

The sudden realisation took her breath away. She was in love with Seth, It didn't seem possible. Yet somewhere along the way this enigmatic man, who'd faced both poverty and tragedy and risen above them to make a successful life for himself on the other side of the world, had irrefutably started to knock down the barriers she'd built round her heart.

Not wanting to alert him to her feelings, Imogen quickly changed tack. 'I'm not denying that I'm attracted to you in that way. And I'm sorry I said what I did. I suppose I'm just feeling stressed about the wedding tomorrow. You're probably right. We should both forget about the past and concentrate on the future. From tomorrow we'll be starting a new life together. We don't want to start out being at loggerheads, do we?'

Low voiced, he agreed, 'No. We don't.'

His hands slid away from her and he stepped back. Straight away Imogen realised that he regretted not letting passion sweep them away. The heat between them seemed to be even more palpable now, after she'd vented her feelings. He was even more frustrated.

Greg's impatience and frustration with her had ended up driving him into another woman's arms. Would that be the outcome if she didn't please Seth in that way, due to her lack of experience? Did he still intend to make love to her on their wedding night? she wondered anxiously. More important, would he remember that it would be her first time?

'By the way,' he added, not quite meeting her eyes, 'I've arranged to sleep in another room down the hall tonight. I think it's best. There are some phone calls I need to make, and you're going to need some privacy to prepare for the wedding. I've asked Celia Bamford to call on you in the morning, to help you with the dress. She'll also be joining us at the ceremony, and at the wedding breakfast afterwards. I've arranged for separate cars to take us to the venue, so we won't be seeing each other until the ceremony. Is there anything else I can do for you before I go?'

Imogen wished she could say, *Yes...I need you to look at me as if I'm important to you and not distance yourself as you're doing now.* Instead, she answered, 'No, there's nothing. It sounds as if you've taken care of everything.'

There was a fleeting glimmer of what seemed to be disquiet on his face, but it quickly disappeared. 'In that case I'll say goodnight.'

'Goodnight, Seth.'

She wanted him to take her in his arms and kiss her, to reassure her that everything would work out for the best. But it seemed he had decided to maintain his distance until tomorrow, and after her outburst just now there was nothing she could do about that but accept it...

Rising from the sumptuous bed that she had occupied on her own last night, Imogen glanced out of the window to see that the morning was bright, but likely very cold. A lone leaf skittered across the immaculate lawns that were covered in a veil of icy frost, and the sounds of birdsong seemed muted.

Was it an omen that she would end up alone after all? That Seth wouldn't follow through with the marriage?

Impatient that she still found it so hard to trust, she escaped into the bathroom to take her shower.

When she emerged a while later her gaze immediately fell on the exquisite dress she would be wearing that day. It was draped on a hanger outside the wardrobe, its delicate shimmering folds resembling the magical garb of a mythical princess. But it wasn't at all easy to feel joyful about it. How could she? She was marrying a man who didn't love her and history seemed to be repeating itself.

Would she ever be able to reach Seth's heart and help him see that she had come to believe that love wasn't a mere emotion, that it was the truest thing of all? That if he gave it a chance it would help dissolve the fear of loss that undoubtedly dogged him and allow him to see that he deserved to love and be loved again, by a woman who honestly adored him? Imogen wanted him to know that there *were* second chances in life and that his first love didn't have to be his only one.

With a heartfelt sigh, she moved across to the dressing table to fix her hair...

It had been ten years ago that Seth had started his career in America, and with his knowledge of mechanics and his enthusiasm to work on the most desirable sports cars that career had spectacularly taken off to catapult him into the elite world of the rich and famous. Since then he had experienced many social events amongst the great and the good, but he had never felt more tense or nervous about an occasion as he did now, on the day of his marriage to Imogen.

Last night he'd found out that she wasn't entirely happy with him. Her outburst had seriously given him cause to doubt his decision to marry her. What was she looking for in this upcoming partnership of theirs? Had he missed something?

Because of his disquiet he hadn't enjoyed the best night's sleep. In fact he'd hardly slept at all. He'd been far too restless. Restless and *frustrated*. Dominating his thoughts had been the moment when he would hopefully take her in his arms and make her his own...

As arranged, they were travelling to the Peel Tower in separate cars, so that he wouldn't see his bride before the wedding. Acting as one of their witnesses, the hotel manager sat beside him. He was a friendly young man called Aziz, and with his cheerful upbeat manner he gamely endeavoured to help Seth feel more relaxed.

In truth it was a futile exercise, because he wouldn't relax until he had put his ring on Imogen's finger and officially made her his wife. It was a matter of honour to him. He wanted her to know that not all men were cheats and liars like her ex-fiancé.

On their arrival at the venue, they discovered that the ancient tower was situated amidst a sea of manicured lawns and surrounded by a graceful meadow. The scene was utterly charming for a young bride to see on her wedding day, he mused, and he hoped that Imogen would be delighted by it.

When they'd disembarked from the white Rolls Royce they'd arrived in, the immaculately dressed steward waiting for them directed them inside. Seth and the affable Aziz would wait there for Imogen and the concierge, Nina, to arrive.

As they climbed the age-old stone steps to the room where the ceremony would take place Seth's stomach muscles clenched hard. For the first time since she'd died, all those years ago, he couldn't seem to conjure up Louisa's face. A momentary sense of panic rolled through him. Was he starting to forget her?

As he tussled with the idea, he followed the steward through an arched doorway into a beautiful serene chamber, where it seemed that time had stood still for centuries. The atmosphere was as hushed and reverent as inside a church. But aside from the tangibly almost holy atmosphere, he found that he hardly registered much else. Not even the historical artefacts and paintings on the walls surrounding them claimed his attention as they might have done if he hadn't been about to undertake something as momentous as this marriage.

The anticipation of seeing Imogen again and the fear that she might be regretting making this commitment to him after all wasn't exactly reassuring. Their final words last night had been undeniably awkward and stilted as they'd bade each other goodnight. Seth had been feeling selfishly disgruntled that she hadn't succumbed to a little more intimacy with him, and Imogen had angrily suggested that the deal they'd made was cold and devoid of feeling.

He wanted to reassure her that he genuinely cared about her feelings, and that if it was what she wanted he'd aim to make things up to her by giving her a wedding to remember. He had even relented and had a photographer from a reputable style magazine in attendance, so that he and Imogen would have some pictures to mark the event.

His hope was that she would have some nice memories of their wedding and that they would eventually help make her forget about the humiliation of being jilted at the church by her ex-fiancé, as well as show her family and friends that she was *more* than capable of making good decisions.

He was more than a little stunned when he realised that his feelings for Imogen were becoming disturbingly stronger day by day, hour by hour and moment by moment. Lost in thought, he was jolted when Aziz nudged him.

'Mr Broden?' the other man said quietly. 'Your bride is here.'

Seth turned round and was immediately struck dumb. What confronted him was a vision of the loveliest woman he had ever seen…dressed in the exquisite silk and lace wedding gown he'd bought her. To set off the beauty of the dress Imogen's alluring chestnut curls were crowned by a delicately arranged floral headdress. Against her breast she clutched a small bouquet of ravishing white camellias.

Her incandescent beauty astounded him. She was quite simply *bewitching.* He walked towards her, then dazedly came to a standstill, and for a second or two his words deserted him.

'Hello, Seth.' Her prettily painted coral lips curved in a tentative smile.

'You look utterly enchanting.' Keeping his words low, for her ears only, he went on, 'Just as though you stepped out of a dream.'

He held out his hand and she gracefully accepted it. Any tension that might have previously seized her ebbed away, and her beautiful brown eyes shone like twin candles, lighting the way on a moonlit night.

'You look pretty good, too,' she told him. Her cheeks dimpling, she took her time surveying the flawless grey tuxedo, waistcoat and matching silk tie that he wore. 'Just like a movie star.'

'As long as I please you…that's all that matters, sweetheart.'

An elegant woman dressed in a formal navy blue suit stepped forward just then to introduce herself as the celebrant. She asked, 'Mr Broden? Miss Hayes? Are you ready to be married?'

Seth had told her that she looked as if she'd stepped out of a dream and from that moment on Imogen felt as if she inhabited one. During a beautifully conducted ceremony they made their vows and she officially became Mrs Seth Broden.

Nothing could have been more surreal than the moment when Seth put the diamond-encrusted platinum ring he'd bought on her wedding finger. She only wished she had thought to buy one for him. Would he have minded if it had been a far simpler affair than the one he'd given her?

But then she thought, *Surely love is far more valuable than any jewel or diamond?*

CHAPTER TEN

THE SENSE THAT she must be dreaming stayed with Imogen for the rest of the day—throughout the wedding breakfast that followed and afterwards, when they were toasted with champagne by Celia Bamford, their witnesses, and some of the friendly hotel staff.

She felt as if she was in some kind of trance. Oh, she talked and she smiled at people, and ate some of the incredible food that had been prepared for them, but her ability to remember who, what and where seemed to have deserted her. All she seemed to be able to focus on was Seth. He stayed by her side the whole time, catching her hand if there was the merest hint of her being monopolised by anyone else, and sending her a smile that conveyed to her that this was *their* day. Nothing else would take precedence.

Anyone observing them must believe that theirs was a true love match—that their wedding had come about because they couldn't bear to be without each other. How surprised they'd be if they knew that the ceremony had been instigated out of a purely practical desire to help each other out.

Hurriedly jettisoning the thought—because for today at least she wanted to imagine that Seth *did* love her—Imogen endeavoured to engage with their guests and keep to herself the fact that their supposedly 'convenient' marriage had truly become the most important event of her life...

When they finally departed for their suite she was almost certain that she would suddenly wake up and find herself back in her flat, alone. The charismatic Seth Broden was just a figment of her imagination... He *had* to be, didn't he?

'At last I've got you all to myself Mrs Broden.'

Seth's warm breath tickled her nape as his strong arms went round her waist. He'd captured her from behind and her senses were flooded by his sexy, classy cologne and the irresistible natural scent of the man himself.

'So you have...' she murmured softly.

'You're trembling,' he said, breathing against her hair.

'I know...' There was no point in denying it. The dreamlike events of the day had been overwhelming. Now, alone with her new husband and nervous about what might be following, could anyone blame her for trembling?

Seth turned her in his arms and his compelling blue eyes stared into hers. A sexy half-smile played across his lips. 'Do you want to make love with me, Imogen? I need to know now, before I venture any further.'

Staring back into his eyes, she felt any doubts she might have held on to melt away. Because he'd *asked* her, hadn't just *presumed* they would make love, she was more than reassured that her agreement to go ahead was the right one.

'I do, Seth. I want to make love with you very much.'

He released a long, slow breath. 'That's music to my ears, baby.' The smile he gave her was nothing less than heartfelt. 'And there's no need to be nervous. We're going to take things very slowly. I know it's your first time and I want you to enjoy it.'

'Maybe…maybe I should go and take a shower first?'

He surprised her with a distinctly predatory glance. 'Are you crazy? Taking a shower is the last thing I want you to do. The natural scent of your body turns me on.'

She was already tense with anticipation of the event to come, and his frank remark stunned her to silence. The cool lace of her beautiful gown suddenly became too hot where it glanced against her skin, and inside the fitted bodice her breasts ached and surged.

Swaying against him, she lifted her face. There would be no more words…provocative or otherwise. Instead, Seth's lips came down on hers, hungrily, insatiably, as though he couldn't bear one more second to pass without tasting her. His hands cupped her face and Imogen dizzyingly pressed herself against him, knowing that she wasn't likely to be taking things slowly any time soon. Desire was like a raging river inside her that wouldn't be quelled—not until she was intimately acquainted with his body in the fullest sense possible…

As if echoing her feelings, Seth lifted his mouth from hers, breathing hard. 'I don't want to tear your dress, sweetheart, but if I don't strip it off you soon I'm liable to go crazy.'

Standing on tiptoe, she greedily stole another kiss from him, loving the way it took him by surprise, and felt him eagerly reach for her dress fastening to undo it.

Stilling his hand, she said shakily, 'No. Let me do it.'

As the garment drifted lazily down to her feet it resembled the dying petals of a delicate ivory lily. Stepping out of it, Imogen kicked off her shoes. Next to go was her very feminine and pretty headdress. All she was left wearing was a flimsy ivory-coloured chemise, with white stockings and a matching bra and knickers.

Although she felt incredibly exposed, she also had a sense of being surprisingly free—free from the self-imposed strictures that had so often stopped her from enjoying her life to the full.

Witnessing Seth, sucking in a breath, she watched him breathe it out again slowly. *He couldn't take his eyes off her.* Then, with a distinct economy of effort, he smoothly removed his jacket and tie. Even the rustle of the material was seductive. It was like watching poetry in motion, Imogen thought excitedly. Everything he touched seemed drawn to do his bidding.

She opened her mouth to ask if they should go into the bedroom, but before she could utter the words he lifted her high into his arms and took her there. Carefully setting her down on the luxurious bed, he began to disrobe. Now it was Imogen's turn to feast her gaze.

When Seth was down to black silk boxers, her mouth turned dry. She had already been aware that he was seriously fit and toned, but when she saw him in the flesh she had to stifle a gasp. If she had to describe it, she'd say that his body resembled a sublime Renaissance sculpture come to life. From his lean, hard-muscled biceps to his wide shoulders and slim hips, his musculature was smooth and mouth-wateringly defined.

Aware that she was watching him, he stopped to

push his hand through his tawny hair. It lazily flopped onto his forehead. 'Now it's your turn, sweetheart.'

The low-voiced declaration put her in a spin. 'You mean you want me to undress…completely?' She could barely get the words out.

'Yes—and I want you to let me watch as you do it.'

'Really…? I—I mean, I…' She gulped down a breath 'I suppose under the circumstances I don't have much choice.'

'You *always* have a choice, angel, but I don't doubt you'll make the right one.'

Seth's faith in her wasn't so easy to apply when his helplessly lascivious gaze was studying her so intently.

It took every ounce of courage Imogen had in her to follow through with it, but with a breathy little sigh she started to peel off her stockings. Reminding herself that it was her wedding night, and of how much it meant to her, she took her time and deliberately turned the action into a provocative striptease. To her astonishment, she actually found herself enjoying it. She was no seductress, but she wanted to make their night together memorable, and for Seth not to forget that she'd willingly stripped for him despite not doing it for any other man before.

Inching towards the end of the bed, she felt the silken counterpane beneath her heightening her senses wherever it touched her flesh. She took her time to stretch out the sensual tension between them. When she stood up to remove her chemise Seth's eyes visibly darkened. It was easy to see that he was straining to contain his desire.

With a teasing little smile she continued to undress, as though born to the task. When she'd finally slipped the garment off completely she took off her bra, and stood before him wearing just her lace panties. She didn't cover herself as she might have done but stood proudly, knowing without vanity that he liked what he saw.

Keeping her arms down by her sides, she moved to stand in front of him. 'I thought you might like to help me remove these?' Even as her glance dropped meaningfully down to her underwear her daring made her tremble...

With an enigmatic smile, Seth didn't reply. Instead, he yanked her towards him and ground his lips against hers in a hard, hot kiss. His passionate response might have made Imogen crumple had he not been holding her.

Reclaiming her breath, she remarked softly, 'I take it that means yes?'

'Damn right it means yes, you little witch.'

His big hands possessively cupped her bottom, his palms shaping the smooth soft flesh with undisputed eagerness. Then he impelled her towards him, expertly and seductively easing the delicate lingerie down over her thighs. For a while he just stood and stared, drinking in the sight of her, and even though she was quaking inside Imogen managed to resist crossing her arms to cover herself.

'You're so beautiful it hurts my eyes to look at you, angel...' he commented huskily.

And as his gaze trailed down over her body and back again she felt every single glance as though they were tiny shocks of electricity. Again, time seemed to slow and grow still. Finally, shaking his head as if to free himself from a spell, Seth stood back to remove his boxers. Imogen had another good reason to appreciate his impressive physicality. His manhood was beautifully and unashamedly erect.

Moving away, he drew down the bedcovers, then returned to lift her onto the bed. With bated breath, Imogen found herself lying supine on the silken sheets as she waited impatiently for him to join her.

He didn't keep her waiting long. The air was stirred by the arresting, clean scent of his masculine cologne and the heat from his body as he positioned himself above her and immediately started to rain a series of provocative little kisses all over her face. Finally, leaving his tantalising imprint on her mouth, he bent his head to apply the same provocative attention to her body.

As he suckled her breasts, taking the nipples deep into his mouth and grazing them with his teeth, she whimpered with pleasure. Her desire for him was growing stronger by the second. In fact it was quickly turning into a desperate need that had a mind of its own, and she knew it wouldn't ebb until it was fulfilled...

'I want to make sure that you're properly ready for me, sweetheart.'

Lifting his head, Seth momentarily studied her. His blue eyes blazed with a new kind of intensity now and it made Imogen shiver.

'If you're not, then it's going to hurt.'

'I trust you, Seth,' she replied softly.

'That's good, baby.' He smiled.

His kisses moved further down her body. Each one seared her flesh as though it were a sensuous flame, setting her alight. Of its own volition her body started to tremble. She felt his hands urge her thighs apart, and suddenly her whole world imploded as Seth touched his lips to her most intimate place. She had never known a heat like it.

As he started to kiss her the sensual pleasure inside her built and built, and Imogen writhed and moaned, her hands possessively gripping his hair. When her climax came, it came fast and strong. It was like an urgent, unstoppable tidal wave that drowned her in the most deliciously compulsive heat known to man. So incredible was the sensation, she knew she would never forget it. Tears of emotion welled in her eyes and wouldn't be contained.

Lifting his head to gaze concernedly down at her, Seth asked, 'Are you okay?'

Her voice catching, she said, 'I'm not crying because I'm upset.' Reaching up to touch his face tenderly, she stared at him in wonder. 'I'm crying because what you did was so good. I never knew that intimacy could be like this.'

'Then, are you ready to take things further? Because I'm in serious trouble if you're not.'

'Yes, I am. I promise you I want this as much as you do, Seth.'

'Then, stop talking and kiss me.'

Even though it sounded like a command, Imogen had no intention of resisting. She already knew that her husband's kisses were powerfully addictive and, more than that, she wanted to return some of the pleasure he had given her.

It was a sheer delight to run her hands over his magnificent body and learn which areas were particularly sensitive. In response, he murmured his encouragement, letting her know how every touch and kiss she gave him heightened his enjoyment even more.

The moment came when his passionate admonitions stopped and once again he pressed her slim thighs apart. This time the action had a sense of urgency about it, and she bit down on her lip as he began to insert his erect satin shaft inside her. At first she tensed. And at the very moment his sex delved more deeply and she felt the sting of her hymen being torn she cried out. But he hungrily claimed her lips and the brief discomfort left her.

Very soon they were moving as one. With no more barriers between them their lovemaking intensified, and Imogen gave herself completely to Seth. The second time she peaked the sensations were so powerful they felt as though they rocked her world forever. Her heart was full to bursting with joy. Her body had never felt more alive or more sated.

But her pleasure was so much more than just physical. It reached deep inside her bones and made her blood sing. It told her without a doubt that Seth was the love she'd always hoped for but feared she would never find. What she had felt for her ex was a schoolgirl crush in comparison.

'That was wonderful…' she breathed against his ear, planting a loving kiss at the side of his neck.

Looking up at him, she saw his extraordinary blue eyes boring into hers. Her hands gripped his shoulders and held on tight as he finally came undone with a deep, unforgettable groan.

'I…' He started to say something but stopped to get his breath back and laid his head on her chest instead.

She didn't prompt him to finish what he'd been

going to say. She was simply content just to hold him in her arms, to run her fingers through the silken strands of his hair and revel in the incredible event that had just happened.

But just as she thought he might be feeling the same Seth carefully extricated himself and lay down beside her. With his voice pitched intimately low he breathed, 'Thank you. Thank you for the incredible gift you've just given me.'

The heartfelt declaration momentarily took Imogen aback. 'I'm glad it was important to you, Seth... and I'm glad I waited all these years for the right man to give it to.'

Tracing her lips with the pad of his forefinger, he studied her with a new intensity. '*Am* I the right man, baby?'

As he spoke he carefully examined her luxuriant chestnut hair where it was spread out behind her on the pillow, twining a curl round his finger. The expression on his handsome face was serious.

'What do *you* think?' Imogen wanted to smile, but somehow she found it was beyond her right then. She still feared his rejection if she confessed the *real* reason she'd surrendered her virginity to him—because she loved him. Seth had already warned her that he didn't believe in making emotional attachments.

'Hmm... I think we make a very good match. Don't you? But I have to ask... Do you have any regrets about not giving your virginity to your ex-fiancé?'

'Are you serious?'

'Perhaps deep down you're sad that it wasn't him who was your first lover?'

Imogen was shocked. 'That's ridiculous. I told you—I

don't regret for a moment that things didn't turn out the way I'd hoped. Why would I? It was beyond cruel of him to humiliate me like that. And now I know that he also did me a favour when he didn't turn up that day.'

'So it's true that you really didn't love him after all?'

'Yes, it's true.' She sighed. 'I didn't. Like I told you before, I was only kidding myself about that. When he stood me up at the church I finally realised it was just the *idea* of being in love that I was mesmerised by, and consequently I got my comeuppance.'

'And now... Can you be content with not achieving the dream of *real* love that you wanted, Imogen? Is the pragmatic arrangement we've talked about going to be enough for you?'

As he uttered the words Seth knew without doubt that he no longer wanted such a soulless partnership for himself. He abhorred the very idea. Imogen had invaded his blood with her beauty, her innocence and her wonderful, kind nature, and he would be a fool to pretend that he wanted a marriage of convenience any longer.

Realising the depth of his feelings, he could no longer deny what he *really* wanted from her...

The question he'd asked Imogen made her heart sink. It was suddenly brought home to her that Seth was still pledged to the memory of Louisa...even after all these years. What if that never changed? *Could* she be content with just being his companion? Sharing his bed, but not ever having his love?

Another more startling thought went through her mind just then. *What if they had children?* They'd been swept along with the wedding, and the practicalities of using protection had seemingly gone out of their heads...

Right at that moment she didn't have the courage to ask him about it. It was bad enough to know that he didn't love her.

Her expression grave, she said, 'You're a good man, Seth. I know that. And you've been very frank with me about what you want from the start. So we'll just leave things as they are for now, shall we?'

Unable to disguise her sadness, she swung her legs over the side of the bed and got out, dragging a sheet with her. Winding it round her, she turned away.

Alarmed, and hardly able to believe what he was witnessing, Seth sat up. 'Where do you think you're going?'

'I'd like to take a shower...on my own.'

'Do you really have to do that right now? Why don't you wait and I'll—?'

But she had gone before he'd even realised that she was serious, and she shut the bathroom door with a resounding bang that echoed warningly round the room. He was in no doubt that she was mad at him.

Galvanised into sudden action, Seth dragged the other sheet off the bed and wrapped it round his lean, hard middle. Then he planted himself firmly outside the bathroom and banged hard on the door.

'Imogen! For God's sake, what's going on with you? Do I have to remind you that it's our wedding night?'

The tense moments that passed as he anxiously waited for her response felt like an eternity. Then, in a voice that was barely discernible, she said softly, 'I just need some space for a few minutes. Is that a problem?'

He emitted a frustrated breath and agitatedly pushed

his fingers through his hair. 'Why do you need some space? If there's something bothering you, can't you just come out and talk to me about it?'

'It's probably best if I don't.'

'What the hell does *that* mean?'

The door suddenly opened. Studying him with those big brown eyes of hers, Imogen protectively crossed her arms over the sheet that she'd wound round herself. The gesture made her appear disarmingly fragile. If Seth didn't get to the bottom of this soon he swore he'd go crazy.

'It means that I don't think I can pretend anymore.'

'Pretend about what?'

'About how I feel about things.'

'Then, why don't you *tell* me? Please, Imogen. It's very important to me to know how you feel.'

His natural concern coming to the fore, he reached out his hand to touch her bare shoulder. Once again he was reminded of how exquisitely soft her skin was. Beneath his fingers, she shivered a little.

'I know that your feelings lie with another woman, in another place and time,' she breathed, 'but I want you to know that I love you *now*, Seth…and I can't live a lie and pretend that I don't—no matter what inducements you put in front of me.'

Seth stared at her. His head was spinning. He was incredulous. Imogen apparently believed that he still loved Louisa and would never love anyone else. It took him aback, because he'd known for quite some time that his feelings had changed dramatically.

He hadn't told her because he could hardly believe it himself. But a few minutes ago, when they'd been making love, he'd almost declared what he felt out loud.

Somehow his beautiful, compassionate new wife had found a way into his wounded heart and started to help heal it. His plans for a 'convenient' arrangement had made a serious U-turn.

'First of all, I *don't* still love Louisa. She belongs firmly in the past. I know that for sure. In truth, I started to realise it quite a while ago—even before we met, Imogen, and I fell for you hook, line and sinker. It's *you* that I love. You and *only* you,' he announced, surveying her tenderly.

She was utterly stunned. 'I can hardly believe it. Are you serious? You said in your note to her that you would only ever love *her*. How come you suddenly seem to have changed your mind?'

'Like I said, I started to realise my feelings were changing quite a while ago. But I stupidly told myself that I'd be betraying her if I didn't hold on to them. At the time I wrote what I did I honestly believed I would never love anyone else like I loved her. And as the years went by and I didn't develop any new relationships I believed it must be true.' Seth frowned. 'I convinced myself that love must be a one-time-only deal.'

With her heart in her mouth, Imogen made herself wait for him to continue.

'But you proved me wrong. Imogen. My feelings probably started to change when you showed up at the manor that day, looking like some tender sprite that had emerged out of the woods. You'd walked all the way from town to try to find out who the writer of that note in your book was. How many other people would have done that? Straight away you intrigued me. You showed me that you cared about what had happened to two perfect strangers—that the idea that they'd reunited gave you hope. Although I didn't realise it, the more time I spent with you, and the more I was acquainted with your loving kindness, the more I fell head over heels in love with you.'

'Oh, Seth…do you really mean it? You really do love me?'

He stared back into her incandescent brown eyes and gathered her tenderly into his arms. 'Yes, I do. I'll spend the rest of our lives together proving it to you, so that you need never doubt it. I don't know what I've done to find somebody like you, but I'll never take it for granted. Now, let's go back to bed, shall we?'

Just a few moments later they lay against the pillows together and Seth pulled up the counterpane around them.

Feeling happier than she'd ever felt before, Imogen sighed. 'You know I said that I knew I'd given my virginity to the right man? I was telling you the truth, Seth. I started to fall in love with you not long after I met you.'

They had both removed their sheets, so that they were naked again, and she was stroking her hand up and down his chest as she spoke. Her fingers kept dipping every now and then to the dark column of hair beneath his navel. Already his blood was heading eagerly south…

'In fact I love you so much that I was prepared to go along with your marriage of convenience just so that I could be with you.'

'And yet again put someone else's happiness before your own?'

Appearing genuinely surprised, she stopped stroking him. 'I wouldn't have been unhappy, Seth. I might not have had your love, but I would have known that you respected me, and if all we'd ever had was a close friendship I would have gladly settled for that rather than be without you.'

For a moment he was lost for words. The phrase *my cup runneth over* sprang helpfully to mind, because that was exactly how he felt. It almost didn't seem fair that he'd been given so much. This beautiful, incredible woman had just become his wife, and of all the things he had achieved in life this was undoubtedly the *best*...

CHAPTER ELEVEN

THEY SPENT THE whole of the next morning in bed. Seth had never allowed himself to be so lazy. Most of his life he had worked hard, risen early and gone to bed late. Even when he'd started to earn good money he hadn't rested on his laurels. He'd worked even harder to increase his bank balance and to make a name for himself in the elite world his customers inhabited.

Determined to stay on top of his game, he had also adopted an unstinting routine to help maintain his health and fitness. In New York he either started his day with an early-morning run or by working out at the gym. But lying there next to Imogen, with the sun pouring in at the window, highlighting her silky bare skin as she lay on her front, he honestly couldn't think of a single thing he'd like to be doing more—except perhaps making love to her again...

As if intuiting that he was watching her, she lifted her head and glanced up at him. With her chestnut curls tumbling sexily over a bare shoulder she had a sleepy-eyed slumberous look that was so alluring. Seth found himself instantly turned on again, despite the fact that they'd made love for most of the night.

'Hey. Are you intending on sleeping the entire day away, Mrs Broden?'

Her cheeks were suffused with indignation, arousing him even more.

'Of course I'm not. I'm going to get up in a minute and see about breakfast. I'm hungry...*ravenous*, in fact.'

'So am I...' Lowering his tone meaningfully, he lay down again.

With a sigh, Imogen turned onto her side to study him. 'Shall we get dressed and go downstairs to the dining room?' she asked, her voice not quite steady.

'Not yet. Food isn't our top priority.'

The lascivious glance he gave her made her emit a husky little groan even before he touched his lips to hers. 'Isn't it?' she breathed.

They both knew she was fighting a losing battle.

'There are a few other needs that I want to see to first,' he insisted. 'Do you *know* how addicted I'm becoming to your body?'

'Mmm-hmm...I think my aches and pains bear that out. Perhaps we were a little too energetic last night? I didn't know I'd be getting in so much practice straight away.'

'You can't beat practice...' Bending his head towards hers, Seth stole a deliberately provocative kiss— the kind of kiss that made his blood turn molten even before he'd finished it. 'And you know what they say about practice...' He slid his hand over her exposed bare breast, loving the way her nipple immediately stood to attention and her dark eyes turned misty.

'What *do* they say?' she breathed softly.

He smiled, knowing it didn't really matter about the answer. This seemingly inconsequential little conversation was definitely only heading one way...

'That it makes even the best things perfect.'

'I don't care about perfection. I want— I just want...'

'What *do* you want, baby?'

'*You*... I just want you.'

To his surprise and delight she manoeuvred herself on top of him and her sultry inner thighs clamped against his sides.

'You've got me,' he said throatily, 'for as long and as often as you want.'

They were enjoying dinner in the restaurant that evening when Imogen remarked, 'By the way, what made you hire a photographer for the wedding? It took me by surprise. I know that you don't exactly court publicity.'

'It seems that I'm changing a lot of my old ways since I met you, sweetheart.' Raising his wine glass to his lips, Seth gave her a tender smile. 'And I hope for the better. I thought it might be nice for you to have some pictures to show to your family and friends. To prove to them that you didn't let what previously happened break you—that you stayed strong and fell in love with a man who adores you.'

Her eyes suddenly awash with tears, Imogen knew her gaze was transfixed. 'I adore you, too, Seth. But I'm a little overwhelmed that you care so much about how I might feel that you would do that for me. I can still hardly believe we're married. I'm scared that I'll suddenly wake up and find that I've been having the most fantastical dream.'

Putting his glass down on the table, Seth captured her hand and lifted it to his lips. 'This is no dream, angel. What's happened has happened because it was *meant*. The older I get, the more I believe that universal forces aren't random. I get the sense that events and situations are being carefully orchestrated. When a relationship feels as right as ours does, what else can you put it down to? Anyway...' He planted a warm kiss across her fingers. 'Now that's clear we can start to enjoy our honeymoon.'

'I'm already enjoying it. Even if we went home today it wouldn't matter...just as long as I know we can be together.'

'We're not going home today. My helicopter pilot will be collecting us in the morning to take us to the airport. Then we're boarding a plane to fly to Italy.'

'Italy?'

'Yes. I'm taking you to La Scala in Milan, to see an opera. Before we see the show we'll shop for a suitable outfit for you to wear, and then, when it's over, we'll enjoy some of the very best Italian food in one of my favourite restaurants. After that we'll have three more days in which to please ourselves and enjoy the sights.'

'And then...when we get home...?'

'We'll talk about where we're going to live.'

The expression on his riveting handsome features suddenly became serious. There was still an unspoken uncertainty about where they would reside, and sooner or later they were going to have to address that.

Her teeth anxiously chewed down on her lip. So much had changed for her in a frighteningly short time, and she was having a little trouble acclimatis-

ing herself. Her good fortune seemed to be unrelenting. She could hardly believe that Seth was taking her
to Italy—and to the opera to boot! How had she got
to be so lucky?

And the most exciting thing of all was that they
would soon be living together as man and wife. What
could it matter *where* they lived? She would willingly
go wherever he did, confident that she would be able
to adapt to a new place or even country if she had to.
The main thing was that they loved each other. That
was what would sustain them. Imogen had once agreed
to become just his companion and helpmate, but now
she was his friend and lover, too...

'It all sounds wonderful. And I'm very much looking forward to discussing where we're going to live
when we get home. You can even move in with me
and give up your hotel suite until we find somewhere
more permanent, if you'd like? I promise my bed is a
lot more comfortable than the couch.'

'I don't doubt that it is—especially if you were in
it with me sweetheart... But there's no need for that.
We'll come up with a solution, I promise.' The glance
he gave her was both steady and reassuring. 'In the
meantime, let's drink a toast to our future.'

Raising her glass, Imogen smiled confidently. 'To
our future... May it be a fruitful and happy one.'

Their first outing in Milan was to the glamorous array
of shops in the Galleria, known to be one of the world's
oldest shopping malls. And it was there that Seth insisted Imogen shopped to buy a dress to wear to the
opera.

The incredible four-storey arcade that was topped

with a distinctive glass dome housed the fashions
of the most elite haute couture designers, Armani,
Dolce & Gabbana and Prada to name just a few, and
it wasn't easy to take it all in. For Imogen, the sight of
so much glitz and glamour under one roof was nothing less than intimidating. It was so far away from the
world she was used to that it might as well have been
on another planet.

Even more intimidating was the prevalence of so
many beautiful and attractive people. Everyone looked
like a model or a movie star. Observing both the men
and the women, she saw they looked to be gliding from
store to store as if born to the task. And every now and
then somebody would stop to take a call on the latest
designer phone, or to take a 'selfie' with a friend and
smile and gesticulate as if it were their divine right
to have such good fortune and not be concerned with
very much else.

And of all the scents that pervaded the area the scent
of money was the strongest perfume of all, she noted.

Realising that this was the world she'd married into,
that like it or not, she was going to have to quickly get
used to it. As astute as ever, her husband straight away
sensed her disquiet.

Guiding her towards the store of one of most famous
designers in the world, he examined her searchingly
with his glittering blue eyes. 'You're far too quiet for
my liking. That tells me you're not enjoying yourself.
Why?'

Glancing uncomfortably at the beautifully dressed
window in front of her, Imogen flushed and uneas-
ily brushed her hand down the faux leather jacket she
wore with jeans. 'I don't want to sound like a broken

record, Seth, but I'm just not used to this kind of thing. It's going to take me a while to adjust.'

'Why? If it's because you don't feel "good enough" to go into such an elite store, let me reassure you. Whether you're married to me or not, you have as much right as the next person to go into this store and have an assistant serve you. And if I detect for even a second that anyone is making you feel uncomfortable, either by a look or a condescending attitude, I'll make sure that I never buy from that designer again. In my world, Imogen, money and status is power. Never forget that. So work on losing that demoralising feeling and enjoy yourself. Now let's go in and find you a beautiful dress to wear to the opera.'

Brushing her lips with an affectionate kiss, Seth caught her hand and led her into the store, and Imogen loved him all the more for his insistence that she was as deserving as anybody else to shop there...

La Scala was an unbelievable experience from the moment their car dropped them off at the square.

The deceptively unprepossessing building turned out to contain an Aladdin's cave of wonder and delight. Inside the auditorium, with its six perfect 'doll's house' tiers, the atmosphere was somehow imbued with the echoes of all the magnificent voices that had ever sung there...indeed, that sang there still. The members of the audience who had started to fill the seats were immaculately dressed and important looking. The men wore flawless suits and the women were dressed in an array of classic and fashionable gowns practically dripping with jewels.

Although she and Seth talked amongst themselves

Imogen was so mesmerised by the fact that she was there at all that she hardly knew what she said. And when they finally took their seats in one of the most desirable boxes in the theatre, she honestly attested to feeling like the fairy tale Cinderella must have done when she went to the ball.

Seth held her hand and every now and then discreetly pointed out an important official or celebrity that he'd spotted, adding an amusing anecdote or two if it was someone he had met personally.

One of the best things of all about that magical day was the sensational scarlet gown that Seth had helped her choose. It was simply glamour personified, and she couldn't deny that she felt like a different woman wearing it—a woman who was confident and assured. And adding to that rare sense of confidence was the fact that she was with Seth.

Her handsome husband had caused a small sensation when he'd stepped out of their car, because he looked so amazing in yet another classy Armani suit. The owners of the high-lens cameras that had pointed in their direction attested that it hadn't gone unnoticed who he was. Coupled with that, there had been several times when some of the most stunning women Imogen had ever seen had glanced admiringly his way. But she didn't let it disturb her. After all, *she* was the one he'd made his wife.

The opera that evening was *La Bohème*, by Puccini, and the powerful emotive music stayed with her long after they'd returned to their hotel. In truth, neither of them wanted the magic to end, and that night Seth took his time making slow, sweet love to her. It was the icing on the cake in an extraordinarily happy day that would be etched in her memory forever.

The following few days saw them touring several art galleries and other places of interest, but Imogen's favourite thing was their visit to the church of Santa Maria delle Grazie, to see Leonardo Da Vinci's *The Last Supper*. Although she could see that the incredible painting had faded down the years, it was still powerfully moving. Seth was right. There was so much about Italy that was utterly compelling.

On their return to the hotel the day after their final lunch in town Seth took himself off to the bathroom for a shower. Contentedly lying on the bed, browsing through a magazine, she was finally distracted by the persistent message tone of his phone. He'd left it on the bed, down by Imogen's feet, and although she wouldn't normally dream of looking at it, it came to her that it might be something urgent.

Gathering up the smartphone, she stared down at the name that had appeared on the screen. Not recognising it as anyone he'd mentioned, she scrolled further down to read the message.

Well, my friend, have you found your trophy wife yet? My father the sheikh is anxious to meet you with a view to making you his new supplier. I'm sure you know what an amazing opportunity this is. We're talking about entry into the 'elite of the elite' classic-car fraternity and you need to have a wife to make you eligible. Don't let your reticence about making this marriage one of convenience deter you much longer! You know it makes sense. Ring me. Ash.

In those horrific few moments as the words seeped into her brain Imogen felt as if time had chillingly slowed down in order to manifest the nightmarish re-alisation that now seized her.

Her husband had been lying to her all along about his reasons for marrying her.

Tightening her hold on the mobile, she reread the message. She hadn't made a mistake... The words were writ clear in black and white.

The glossy magazine she'd been so avidly perusing just a moment ago slid off the bed and landed on the floor. Shock, dizziness and sickness infiltrated her in-sides all at once. Dear God, what was going on? Had Seth just pretended that he loved her? Had their mar-riage been forged purely out of his desire to become a member of this so-called 'elite of the elite' frater-nity, and was *she* the 'trophy wife' his friend had sug-gested he find?

If it was true, then Imogen knew it would be a far worse betrayal than Greg's had ever been.

Throwing the phone down on the bed as if it was some kind of dangerous explosive device, she hurriedly moved to stand in front of the large ornate window that overlooked the piazza. Although the square still teemed with people, Imogen barely registered the fact. Her heart was thumping so hard it made it nigh on im-possible for her to think straight.

Right at that moment Seth reappeared. He had a single white towel wrapped round his toned middle and his damp hair was tousled from what must have been a cursory attempt at drying it. His blue eyes au-tomatically seeking her out, he gave her one of his usu-ally irresistible smiles. But this time, Imogen was in

no mood to be charmed by it. She was far too angry...
angry and confused.

'What exactly is a trophy wife, Seth?' She was endeavouring to keep her tone cool, but it didn't prevent
her from shaking inside as she asked the question. 'I
hope you can enlighten me, because I'm anxious to
know.'

He stopped smiling. 'What on earth are you talking about?'

She jerked her head towards the mobile she'd thrown
down onto the bed. 'You had a message from someone
who clearly knows you much better than I do. I didn't
mean to read it, but I'm glad that I did.'

Not commenting, he immediately reached for the
device. As he read what was on the screen his counte-
nance visibly paled. Then he swore under his breath.
Was that a sign that he was guilty of the very thing she
had dreaded? Imogen wondered sickeningly.

Jettisoning the phone, Seth deliberately walked towards her. 'Reading that, I can understand why you no
doubt believe I lied to you about my motives for marrying you. All I can tell you, Imogen, is that it's not true.
I married you purely because I love you and could not
contemplate living my life without you.'

When he would have stepped closer she folded her
arms over her chest and stared at him coldly. It wasn't
easy to stem her suspicions that he was lying. She was
honestly terrified of being so gullible a second time.

'If that's so, then what's all that about you needing
to find a trophy wife to enter this sheikh's "elite of the
elite" classic-car fraternity?'

'That part is true, in that my friend Ash recommended me to him. It's his father who is ruler of a king-

dom with a very ancient history, and his wealth is much envied and admired. The sheikh is an avid classic-car collector and is reported to have the richest collection of classic cars in the world. To be accepted into that fraternity you need to be married as well as rich, because they have a very traditional culture.'

Pausing to take a breath, Seth dragged his hand through his hair.

'When I met you I suggested us having a marriage of convenience partly because it would help me to be accepted into that fraternity. I also saw that we could genuinely help each other out because we had both been disappointed in love. But I also quickly began to realise that I was falling for you. When I married you that day at Gretna Green, Imogen, it was the happiest day of my life. I no longer care about becoming the sheikh's new supplier of elite cars. In fact I'm going to text my friend today and let him know I decline the offer. The only thing I really care about now is *you*.'

Although his declaration made her heart sing, she was still anxious about it blinding her to the truth. 'I want to believe you,' she confessed shakily, 'but I'm so scared of being taken for a fool again. Right now I just don't know what to believe.'

'Maybe I can do something to help you?'

'What?'

'Let's go and sit down and I'll show you.'

Waiting for her to make the first move. Seth followed her back to the bed, then gestured for her to sit down. When she did, he once more picked up his phone and sat next to her. He efficiently pressed a couple of buttons and a photo of someone called Ash Nassar appeared on the screen. He had tanned skin and a fashionably short haircut.

The number started ringing, and when it was answered her husband declared, 'Hi, Ash, it's Seth. I'm in Italy on my honeymoon and I've only just read your message.'

'Seth—it's about time! I wondered what the delay was. So you took my advice and found yourself a trophy wife? You couldn't have timed it better. How soon can you travel over here to seal the deal? My father has already told me that if you marry the job is yours.'

'I appreciate all your efforts on my behalf, my friend…but I'm afraid I'm going to have to decline the offer.'

'Tell me you're joking? Do you realise this is the kind of opportunity that only comes along once in a lifetime—if that? Tell me the truth. Has someone tempted you with something better?'

His lips breaking into a smile, Seth glanced at Imogen and clasped her hand. He had put the call on speakerphone and knew she had heard every word. Thankfully the look of dread in her glossy brown eyes had started to fade…

'Yes,' he replied. 'They have.'

'I can hardly believe it. Who *is* he?'

'The person concerned isn't a man. She's a woman. As a matter of fact she's my *wife*, and her name is Imogen. As important as it is to you and your father, it's no longer important to *me* to acquire the kudos of being accepted into your family's world, Ash. With respect, I don't need that kind of acceptance. And neither do I need the business or the even richer trappings that come along with it. I'm successful enough in my own right. What I want and need most is my beautiful wife and the amazing new life we're going to make together.'

Again, he directed a warm smile at Imogen.

'And if I were you I'd take your own advice and get yourself a wife... Find a woman you can truly love with all your heart. I've discovered that that's the most valuable treasure of all, my friend.'

At the other end of the phone, all was silent. Then, just when Seth thought his friend had disconnected, he heard him chuckle.

'You sound as if you are truly smitten!'

Gazing back at Imogen, he nodded. 'I am. When you next come over to the UK, I'll introduce you to her.'

'That's a deal. By the way—does this rose amongst the daisies have a sister?'

CHAPTER TWELVE

AFTER THEY'D KISSED and made up, following the most tumultuous episode of their marriage so far, Imogen didn't think her feet touched the ground until the morning they boarded their plane back to London.

But then, home again as their plane touched down at Heathrow, she started to feel nervous for another reason. All of a sudden their joyful wedding in Scotland and their trip to Italy seemed light years away, and to a certain degree she knew she would have to come back down to earth. She couldn't let her taste of the high life blind her to the inevitable practicalities of life. And nor could she help dreading the moment that she and Seth would have to say goodbye to each other for a while.

They still hadn't decided where they were going to live, and she presumed she'd be returning to the flat until they did. She hardly relished the idea of being apart from him for too long.

When Seth steered the smart sedan he'd rented at the airport down the street where she lived and parked it outside her door, for a long moment they both fell silent.

Twisting the beautiful diamond-encrusted wedding ring round her finger, Imogen formed her lips into a shaky smile. 'Want to come in for a coffee before you head back to the hotel?' she asked.

'No, angel. I want you to pack the bare essentials and come with me. And before we return to the hotel together I'm going to take you to see a house.'

'You mean you've found somewhere already?'

'Wait and see,' he told her.

Now Imogen's nerves escalated for another reason. Whilst access to the internet had allowed Seth to scan suitable properties even while they were away, and he had informed contacts who could also help, he had barely left her side long enough to investigate.

There was only one vacant house she knew of in the area that could possibly meet his requirements, and he already owned it. It was the magnificent Gothic manor where she had first met him, and it had once been the home of his tragic ex-girlfriend...

Her suspicions proved to be right. When Seth directed the car onto the manor's stately gravelled drive she didn't comment right away. In the dappled afternoon sunlight the architecture of the building was indisputably grand. Its pointed arched roofs reached high into the sky, as if to denote that it was both lofty and important. Her first summation of the building hadn't changed—it was intimidating in more ways than one.

'Why have we come here, Seth? You told me when we first met that you weren't even sure that you'd move in to the house.'

He rubbed at his brow thoughtfully. 'I wasn't. But I've been seriously thinking about it while we were away. It's not as intimidating as it seems. Most of the rooms are spacious, light and airy, and the interior can be transformed into any style we want. The acreage is vast. It would be perfect to entertain business guests from abroad, and for garden parties in the summer.' For a moment he stopped talking to contemplate her. 'And, when we have them, it would also be a perfect place for our children to grow up.'

Imogen's heart thundered inside her chest. They hadn't taken precautions when they'd made love, and they'd been intimate many times since the wedding, so she shouldn't be surprised that the subject had come up. If Seth was all for the idea, then nothing would please her more than to have his children—but to raise them in this house...? She owned to feeling uneasy about that.

'I would love us to have a family, Seth, I really would. But I'm not sure I could be happy living here.'

His dark brows drew together in surprise. 'Why not? You haven't even had a proper look round yet.'

Twisting her hands together in her lap, she knew her glance couldn't hide her misgivings. 'There are too many ghosts here.'

'You're letting your imagination run away with you.'

'No, I'm not.' Imogen sucked in a steadying breath. 'I'm not talking about the traditional kind of ghosts that haunt old buildings and show up in horror stories. I'm talking about the psychological ghosts of Louisa and her family. You're already haunted by them, and now you want us to start our new life together in what was once their home.'

A flash of frustration crossed Seth's vivid blue eyes. 'I'm not haunted by them...not anymore. I've laid all my ghosts from the past to rest. I'm simply looking at the house as an asset, Imogen, that's all. We need some-where to live and we've got this place readymade. I'd be a fool to turn my back on it and sell it to somebody else, and I haven't made a success of my business by *not* capitalising on my advantages.'

'And it wouldn't remind you of Louisa to live here?'

'I hardly even set foot in the place when she was here. Her father didn't think me good enough.'

'But you've got some painful memories of your deal-ings here, haven't you? Can you really forget about them so easily? Do you think a fresh coat of paint and some smart new furniture is enough to permanently dim the memories?'

Seth stared back into the deep brown eyes he so loved and scowled. He knew she had a point. Perhaps it wouldn't be as easy as he'd thought to banish his past associations with the house if they lived there. But what was wrong with at least giving it a try? Prac-ticalities aside, they needed somewhere to move into sooner rather than later—because as comfortable as it was, the luxurious hotel he was staying in wasn't a home. And right now Seth *yearned* to have a home of his own with his wife...

'I'm not saying it has to be for good. But we can at least move in temporarily until we find somewhere else. Please think about it, Imogen.'

'Even a temporary move might prove to be too pain-ful. And I don't mean just for you, Seth, but for me, too.'

'I don't understand...'

'No? Then, why don't you take some time to think it over? In the meantime I'll go back to my flat and check that I haven't forgotten anything. You don't have to give me a lift. It's a lovely day and the walk will do me good.' Opening the passenger door, she got out of the car.

Stunned and aggrieved, Seth could hardly believe his eyes. It honestly disturbed him that he didn't understand her feelings. What did she mean by saying it would be too painful for *her* to move into the manor? She hadn't even known Louisa.

He sat in the car for a long time after she'd left. Then he got out and walked across to the house. Letting himself in, he stepped inside the cavernous hall. The place seemed bright and airy, with the sun streaming through the windows, but he wasn't completely reassured.

The powerful memory of James Siddons not accepting him, making him feel worthless on that fateful day when he'd come to ask for his daughter's hand in marriage, hit him like a tidal wave. He was genuinely shocked that the memory was still so vivid. But it was hard to forget being put down when he was so young. It would always linger somewhere in his psyche and catch him unawares should he ever feel remotely vulnerable.

Yet he knew that if he didn't take steps to try to change that his past would always haunt him. With Imogen by his side, he was certain he could create new and happier memories, and would soon forget his past sorrows. It was like being given the most priceless gift. He realised that his attention was now firmly on the present, and on his hopes for making the best life imaginable with his beautiful new wife. It would be Seth's lifelong mission to make Imogen happy…as happy and thrilled as *he* was that she was the woman he loved. The only woman he would *ever* love from now on…

He took one last look round and then firmly closed the door. Even before he reached the car it came to him just *why* Imogen hadn't taken to the idea of living at the manor. Whilst he still hoped to win her round about that, he could hardly wait to get back to her flat and share his realisation with her...

Before Imogen unpacked she decided to take a quick shower. Beneath the hot, invigorating spray, she mulled over the events of the day, feeling tense at the idea that Seth *still* didn't know why she should be so unsure about his suggestion to live at the manor.

After all, it was the kind of house that most ordinary people could only fantasise about living in. To his mind, it probably didn't make sense that she wouldn't want to live there. No matter what changes had come about he was still pragmatic—a man who utilised his advantages—and he had told her more than once that his practice was not to involve his emotions. That most definitely wasn't the case as far as his relationship with *her* was concerned, but her reasons for not wanting to live at the impressive Gothic house *were* mostly emotional ones.

Sighing, she knew she shouldn't worry so much about sharing her feelings with him. Didn't he often tell her—not just tell her but *show* her—how much he loved and adored her? That being the case, they would be able to come to an amicable conclusion about the manor, she was sure...

After finishing drying herself, she pulled on her bathrobe. She'd just turned on the hairdryer when someone banged on the door. *It had to be Seth.* Barefoot, and naked under her robe, she dashed into the hallway to see if she was right. The shadowy outline outside the door's glass panels confirmed that she was.

'You weren't as long as I thought you'd be,' she declared with a smile. No matter what her feelings about the house, she knew she couldn't remain at odds with him about it for long. She just loved the man too much.

Stepping inside, Seth immediately pulled her into his arms. 'Are you naked under this robe?' he challenged huskily.

'I am. I've just had a shower.'

'Have you, indeed? Then you have to pay the price.'

'What price is that, exactly?' Endeavouring to look demure, Imogen pouted.

'Come into the bedroom and you'll find out.'

'Before we do that, will you tell me what you've decided to do about the manor?'

At the side of Seth's chiselled jaw a muscle flinched, and suddenly he looked serious again. 'We need to talk about that. Will you listen to what I've got to say?'

'Of course.'

Imogen was on tenterhooks as they returned to the living room. Dropping down onto the couch, she fastened the belt of her robe a little tighter round her waist.

'I think I've figured out why you aren't enamoured about living there.'

'Oh?'

As he lowered himself down beside her Seth's gaze was candid. 'You didn't want either of us to be constantly reminded of Louisa and to have it impinge on our happiness. But in all honesty it *wouldn't*. It turns out that it was the memory of her father that troubled me the most. He thought himself superior to anyone who wasn't from the same class as him and, as I told you before, he could hardly wait to let me know that I wasn't good enough. How could I be when I came from the "wrong" side of town? You might find it hard to believe, but even after all these years, and having made a success of my career, I've never forgotten the taunts he threw at me. That's why I bought the house. I wanted to get back at him and prove that I wasn't just good enough…I was *better*.'

'And has it helped you to do that?'

'When I went back there today, and went inside, I confess the memory of him was sharper than I'd realised, and at first it didn't help. But thinking things over and taking the emotion out of it—' his lips shaped an ironic smile '—I also realised that that could change. Not by my walking away from the painful memories associated with the house, but by changing them into better ones. I can't do that on my own, Imogen, but with you by my side I feel like anything is possible.'

She felt so many emotions all at once that she scarcely knew how to voice them. But as soon as she was caught in the beam of Seth's loving gaze she said simply, 'Do you know just how much I love you?'

He lifted his arm to glance teasingly down at his Rolex. 'I'm hoping that in a very short time you'll leave me in no doubt and show me. But first I want to know if you'll consider moving into the manor with me and making it our home.'

All her doubts vanishing, Imogen nodded. 'I will,' she said. Then she tenderly wound her arms round her husband. 'And I want you to know that everything's going to be wonderful. Let the bad memories of the past go, Seth. You have nothing left to prove to anyone. This is going to be a new life for both of us…a fresh start at something important that's been denied us up until now. Let's leave all the sad old memories behind and live in the present. But that doesn't mean we shouldn't hope for a bright future, too. You mentioned children? Well, that features in *my* hopes for the future, too.'

Seth's beautiful sculpted mouth curved in the most melting smile she'd ever seen.

'Then, there's no time like the present to start creating them—is there, Mrs Broden?' he suggested.

And taking her by the hand, he lovingly led her into the bedroom…

EPILOGUE

IMOGEN STEPPED EXTRA carefully down the grand old staircase that had been faithfully restored to display its gracious beauty in all its splendour.

One of the best things about moving into the manor was the opportunity it had given her to indulge in her secret longing to practise interior design. As avant-garde as she could be sometimes, she'd always loved homemaking. And as much as she had genuinely loved her job at the legal practice, designing and choosing interiors for her new home beat it hands down…no question.

Everywhere she rested her eyes, both inside the house and in its extensive gardens, incandescent beauty and love were reflected back at her. Between them, she and Seth had created the most wonderful home. Long gone were the sad old memories that had clung there before.

They had renovated the house up to the rafters. Where before the interior had epitomised the faded grandeur of a bygone age, it now displayed a pleasing mix of modernity along with the more traditional. Restful colour merged with the vibrant furniture and fittings they'd chosen, and every now and then some beautifully classic antiques made themselves evident.

As she neared the end of the staircase Imogen reflected smilingly that these days Evergreen was truly a joy to come home to.

'Stop right there,' instructed the familiar deep bass voice of her husband.

Seth came into the hall from the drawing room, where he'd been looking through the latest designs Imogen had created. She'd left her drawings strewn over one of the larger mahogany tables when he'd firmly told her to go and lie down.

'I thought I told you to take a rest?' He frowned.

'I'm too excited. How am I supposed to rest when my mind's teeming with ideas for new designs and the baby's due any day now?'

Dropping his hands to his hips, in the slim-fitting jeans he wore with a polo shirt, her husband lifted his eyebrows. 'And that's precisely why you should be resting—because the baby's due, not because you're thinking about new designs.'

Shaking his head, Seth approached the staircase and Imogen stood stock-still. Yes, she was eager to get back to her designing, but she never got tired of any excuse to gaze lovingly at her handsome husband. Having his baby was the most wonderful, fulfilling thing that had ever happened to her…next to his declaration that he loved her, of course.

'Are you cross with me?' she teased.

'As if…'

Resting his hands against her waist, he lifted a hand to smooth back a straying chestnut curl from her forehead. It gave her a delightful whiff of his sexy cologne and her hormones went crazy...

'You're far too important for me to stay angry with you for long,' he breathed. 'But seriously, you need to be sensible, sweetheart. You're carrying something very precious to me in there.'

His hands were suddenly on her rounded belly, and the heat from them added to the heat from the baby in her womb and made her heart suddenly race.

'You're very precious to me, too, Seth.' She smiled and dropped a soft kiss on his lips. 'And I promise I'll go and rest if you agree to come with me.'

'Decisions, decisions...' he mocked gently. 'What's a guy to do when the woman in his life makes a command and he wants to stay in her good books?'

Dimpling, Imogen answered, 'That's easy. Just do as she says and do it smartly—especially when she's pregnant!'

'There's no arguing with that, my love.'

Seemingly with no effort at all, Seth scooped her up in his arms and purposefully carried her up the stairs. And as he went the warmest glow of satisfaction and pleasure filled his heart—because now, after all the years he had felt alone, he truly knew himself to be the luckiest man in the world. At last he had found the love he had always longed for...

* * * * *

MILLS & BOON®
Hardback – March 2016

ROMANCE

The Italian's Ruthless Seduction	Miranda Lee
Awakened by Her Desert Captor	Abby Green
A Forbidden Temptation	Anne Mather
A Vow to Secure His Legacy	Annie West
Carrying the King's Pride	Jennifer Hayward
Bound to the Tuscan Billionaire	Susan Stephens
Required to Wear the Tycoon's Ring	Maggie Cox
The Secret That Shocked De Santis	Natalie Anderson
The Greek's Ready-Made Wife	Jennifer Faye
Crown Prince's Chosen Bride	Kandy Shepherd
Billionaire, Boss...Bridegroom?	Kate Hardy
Married for their Miracle Baby	Soraya Lane
The Socialite's Secret	Carol Marinelli
London's Most Eligible Doctor	Annie O'Neil
Saving Maddie's Baby	Marion Lennox
A Sheikh to Capture Her Heart	Meredith Webber
Breaking All Their Rules	Sue MacKay
One Life-Changing Night	Louisa Heaton
The CEO's Unexpected Child	Andrea Laurence
Snowbound with the Boss	Maureen Child

0216 GEN STD HB

MILLS & BOON®
Large Print – March 2016

ROMANCE

A Christmas Vow of Seduction	Maisey Yates
Brazilian's Nine Months' Notice	Susan Stephens
The Sheikh's Christmas Conquest	Sharon Kendrick
Shackled to the Sheikh	Trish Morey
Unwrapping the Castelli Secret	Caitlin Crews
A Marriage Fit for a Sinner	Maya Blake
Larenzo's Christmas Baby	Kate Hewitt
His Lost-and-Found Bride	Scarlet Wilson
Housekeeper Under the Mistletoe	Cara Colter
Gift-Wrapped in Her Wedding Dress	Kandy Shepherd
The Prince's Christmas Vow	Jennifer Faye

HISTORICAL

His Housekeeper's Christmas Wish	Louise Allen
Temptation of a Governess	Sarah Mallory
The Demure Miss Manning	Amanda McCabe
Enticing Benedict Cole	Eliza Redgold
In the King's Service	Margaret Moore

MEDICAL

Falling at the Surgeon's Feet	Lucy Ryder
One Night in New York	Amy Ruttan
Daredevil, Doctor...Husband?	Alison Roberts
The Doctor She'd Never Forget	Annie Claydon
Reunited...in Paris!	Sue MacKay
French Fling to Forever	Karin Baine

MILLS & BOON®
Hardback – April 2016

ROMANCE

The Sicilian's Stolen Son	Lynne Graham
Seduced into Her Boss's Service	Cathy Williams
The Billionaire's Defiant Acquisition	Sharon Kendrick
One Night to Wedding Vows	Kim Lawrence
Engaged to Her Ravensdale Enemy	Melanie Milburne
A Diamond Deal with the Greek	Maya Blake
Inherited by Ferranti	Kate Hewitt
The Secret to Marrying Marchesi	Amanda Cinelli
The Billionaire's Baby Swap	Rebecca Winters
The Wedding Planner's Big Day	Cara Colter
Holiday with the Best Man	Kate Hardy
Tempted by Her Tycoon Boss	Jennie Adams
Seduced by the Heart Surgeon	Carol Marinelli
Falling for the Single Dad	Emily Forbes
The Fling That Changed Everything	Alison Roberts
A Child to Open Their Hearts	Marion Lennox
The Greek Doctor's Secret Son	Jennifer Taylor
Caught in a Storm of Passion	Lucy Ryder
Take Me, Cowboy	Maisey Yates
His Baby Agenda	Katherine Garbera

MILLS & BOON®
Large Print – April 2016

ROMANCE

The Price of His Redemption	Carol Marinelli
Back in the Brazilian's Bed	Susan Stephens
The Innocent's Sinful Craving	Sara Craven
Brunetti's Secret Son	Maya Blake
Talos Claims His Virgin	Michelle Smart
Destined for the Desert King	Kate Walker
Ravensdale's Defiant Captive	Melanie Milburne
The Best Man & The Wedding Planner	Teresa Carpenter
Proposal at the Winter Ball	Jessica Gilmore
Bodyguard...to Bridegroom?	Nikki Logan
Christmas Kisses with Her Boss	Nina Milne

HISTORICAL

His Christmas Countess	Louise Allen
The Captain's Christmas Bride	Annie Burrows
Lord Lansbury's Christmas Wedding	Helen Dickson
Warrior of Fire	Michelle Willingham
Lady Rowena's Ruin	Carol Townend

MEDICAL

The Baby of Their Dreams	Carol Marinelli
Falling for Her Reluctant Sheikh	Amalie Berlin
Hot-Shot Doc, Secret Dad	Lynne Marshall
Father for Her Newborn Baby	Lynne Marshall
His Little Christmas Miracle	Emily Forbes
Safe in the Surgeon's Arms	Molly Evans

MILLS & BOON®

Why shop at millsandboon.co.uk?

Each year, thousands of romance readers find their perfect read at millsandboon.co.uk. That's because we're passionate about bringing you the very best romantic fiction. Here are some of the advantages of shopping at www.millsandboon.co.uk:

* **Get new books first**—you'll be able to buy your favourite books one month before they hit the shops

* **Get exclusive discounts**—you'll also be able to buy our specially created monthly collections, with up to 50% off the RRP

* **Find your favourite authors**—latest news, interviews and new releases for all your favourite authors and series on our website, plus ideas for what to try next

* **Join in**—once you've bought your favourite books, don't forget to register with us to rate, review and join in the discussions

Visit **www.millsandboon.co.uk**
for all this and more today!